I0690604

Impossible Love

First Edition

Published by The Nazca Plains Corporation
Las Vegas, Nevada
2009

ISBN: 978-1-935509-45-5

Published by

The Nazca Plains Corporation ®
4640 Paradise Rd, Suite 141
Las Vegas NV 89109-8000

PUBLISHER'S NOTE
Impossible Love is a work of fiction created wholly by *Hank Brooks'* imagination. All characters are fictional and any resemblance to any persons living or deceased is purely by accident. No portion of this book reflects any real person or events.

Cover Photo, Frenk Kaufmann
Art Director, Blake Stephens

Dedication

This novel is dedicated to all of you who are buried
deep in the closet, and living life in hell.

Impossible Love

First Edition

Hank Brooks

Chapter One

I was dreaming. I had to be dreaming because everything was disjointed. Events were flashing before me, but they were all out of sequence. I couldn't think straight and my head was throbbing. I didn't know where I was or how I had gotten there.

I was vaguely aware that I was sitting in a chair. My rear end was slightly forward and someone was sucking my cock. God, it felt good! Another person was straddling the cocksucker and was forcing his cock into my mouth. I was sucking at it madly. It tasted like honey and I couldn't get enough. Every so often the two men would change positions. Everything would go black from time to time, but when I was aware of my existence, the scene remained the same.

I don't know how long this went on, but after some time I felt my orgasm coming on. I wanted to warn the cocksucker, but my mouth was occupied. Suddenly I felt the familiar taste of warm and salty fluid going down my throat and my own orgasm exploded into the cocksucker's mouth. Ah, how wonderful. I wasn't thinking straight, but I can tell you that this was the most powerful orgasm that I had ever experienced. Then I passed out again.

When I woke up, I was on the floor. My ass throbbed with pain. I knew I had been raped, maybe more than once. The chair was at my side and I reckoned that I had fallen out of it. I was alone. Bright sunshine invaded the room. I was naked and sweating profusely. Even though it was late fall, the room was sweltering. I looked around, but everything was blurry. I couldn't make out where I was. I did see a bed in the room and I crawled over to it. With great difficulty, I climbed onto the bed and passed out again.

I was awakened by a loud knocking on the door and a woman's voice yelling, "Maid Service!"

"Come back later," I screamed as loud as I could. I realized that it wasn't very loud, but the maid did go away. Well, I figured out that I was in a hotel, but I wasn't lucid enough to know who I was or how I had gotten there.

The sun was blazing into the room, and giving me a headache. I got out of bed and drew the blind. Then I walked into the bathroom to relieve myself. While peeing, I realized that there was dried semen all through my pubic hairs and my abdomen. I thought that I must have whacked off and not cleaned up afterward, but then, glimpses of my dream came back to me, and I panicked. IT WAS NO DREAM!

There was a toiletry kit on the counter and I knew instinctively that it was mine. I unloaded it and took out my razor. I shaved and then I showered. With a hotel towel wrapped around me, I went into the room to see if I could find some clothes. I spotted a suitcase on a rack and opened it. It was empty except for airline tickets. I checked the clothes rack and there was nothing there. I was cleaned out.

I looked around the room and saw something lying at the foot of the bed. It was my wallet. I grabbed for it and opened it up. My money and my two credit cards were gone. Fortunately for me, the thieves had left my ID card and my health card. I stared at the ID and slowly everything came back to me.

My name is Jonathan Walters. For whatever reason, everyone calls me Wallie, favoring my surname to my given name. I have been married to my beautiful wife, Marsha for just under two years. I live in Massapequa, NY, and I work for a small marketing company. I am in charge of marketing new products.

Yesterday at 1 PM I took off from LaGuardia Airport to Buffalo, NY to attend a sales and marketing meeting for a new breakfast cereal. My company tries out all our clients' new products in Buffalo. Buffalo is the toughest market in the country. If the product takes off there, it takes off anywhere.

My cab took me downtown to The Sheraton Hotel. I requested a room with a DVD player. Once in my room, I undressed completely. I hung up my suit, shirts and ties, but I left my underwear and socks in my suitcase. I was only staying for two nights. I put my toiletry kit in the bathroom but didn't remove any of its contents. It was 4 PM by the time I had everything in place. It was too early for dinner, and my first meeting was not scheduled until the next morning. I had the whole evening to myself, just as I had planned it. I opened my suitcase. From underneath the contents of the case, I removed a DVD, entitled "Wild Boys and Truckers."

I turned on the TV set and the DVD player, inserted the disc, pushed "play" and got into bed. The action on screen between the hairy older "truckers" and the younger men really turned me on, and I began to stroke my cock. I wanted desperately to cum, but I held back. I had better plans for Mr. Weenie, later this evening.

Are you wondering what a happily married guy is doing watching male porn? Well, I've always known that I was gay, since my sexual fantasies often included some hot boy classmates, but most often I fantasized about some of my even hotter male teachers. Foolishly, I swore not to live a gay life. I determined to marry and live in the mainstream.

I did not have sex with a male until I went to college. In college, I only had very discreet sex with men. I never let myself get involved with any of them, and I only slept with men who lived far distances from me. Those of you, who have been in this position, are aware that the yearnings never leave you, even after marriage; especially after marriage.

I am fortunate to have a job requiring a lot of travel. I have business in many cities, but mostly in Buffalo. Whatever city I find myself in, I know where the gay bars are. I always arrive early and spend my first evening at the bars. I rarely miss getting hooked up for the night. I am now 32 years old. I work out, and my 6 foot frame is fat free. I have jet black hair and steel blue eyes. My cock is uncut and 7 hard inches. If I must say so myself, I am very, very handsome.

When I walk into a bar, men immediately come up to me. They want to buy me a drink or dance with me. I can't afford to be particular. I need the sex fast, because I don't know when the next opportunity will arise. Since I visit Buffalo so often, I found myself breaking my rules for sex. A couple of years ago, I met a guy I know only as Mac. We were immediately attracted to each other. If Mac is at the bar when I come in, it's a given that we will spend the night together. I don't consider that I am getting involved with Mac, but

I do have sex with him several times a year. I think of him often and when I have sex with other men, I fantasize that I am with him.

Last night, I did not spot Mac, but within minutes two young men approached me. They were twins. I got excited. I wondered if I could have sex with them. It would certainly be a first, and I sure wanted to try. They were very young and very handsome, and I wondered if they were jail bait. I reasoned that since they were given entrance to the bar, they must be old enough.

Ryan bought me a drink and Sean asked me to dance. I'm a little old for the gyrations of disco dancing and when we got back to the bar, I was sweating profusely. I gobbled down my scotch and soda instead of sipping it. Within minutes my head was reeling and everything was getting fuzzy. The twins asked where I was staying and offered to take me back to the hotel. That's the last thing I remember, except for the erratic dreams of having sex with both of them. At least the evidence indicated that the sex part was no dream.

The twins had cleaned me out. I didn't even have a pair of underwear. There was nothing I could do but call the desk and tell them that I had been robbed, and that they should call the police. I would then call a business associate and get him to buy me some clothes.

As I reached for the phone, it rang. I picked it up and said, "Hello."

"Wallie!! Where the fuck have you been?" I heard an angry voice ask. It was Tom Baker, the very associate I had intended to ask for help in obtaining clothing. "We've been waiting for you for hours," he continued. I quickly explained that I had gone to a bar last evening for a drink. I neglected to mention it was a gay bar and wondered how I could keep that from the police. I told him that I had been drugged there and that they had taken me back to the hotel and robbed me.

"I just came to, and I was about to call the police," I told him.

"You do that, and I'll be right over," he sounded a lot more sympathetic.

"Tom," I whined. "They took everything. I don't have a stitch of clothing. I need everything from underwear out, even shoes. I'm a size ten."

"I'll take care of everything," he said as he hung up.

I then dialed the front desk, told them what happened and asked them to call the police. I also requested a robe. In minutes a bell boy came with a robe and he informed me that the hotel was sending me lunch. I didn't realize that I had slept through the morning and breakfast. I apologized to the boy

4

for being unable to tip him. I stood up to put on the robe and the towel I was wearing slipped down. I was exposed to the bellboy who smiled at me.

"It's OK Mr. Walters. I know you're good for it. I'll look in on you later to see if there's anything more I can do for you." I didn't imagine it. He winked at me as he left.

Minutes later room service brought me lunch. I told them to put a tip on my tab since I was temporarily without a penny. I didn't realize how hungry I was and I began to gobble down the meal when two detectives arrived. One was fat, balding and middle aged. The other was young, handsome and Mac. I nearly flipped when I saw him and so did he. I had no clue that Mac was a police officer.

There were two chairs in the room. The two policemen each took a chair and I sat on the bed. Mac was sitting in the chair I had been raped on. They asked the usual preliminary questions, name, address, age etc. and finally when that was all done, I was able to tell the story. I felt it was essential to name the bar. I definitely saw the older man sneer. Mac didn't move a muscle on his face. I omitted the fact that sex had been a factor in the robbery, and neither of them pursued that aspect.

When I was done they told me that they would question the bartender to see if he knew who the twins might be, but they were sure the bartender would draw a blank. As they left, Mac said to me. "Try to remember anything else which might help us and I'll be back later to check on you."

About a half hour after Mac left, Tom came in. He is about an inch shorter than I, but otherwise we are pretty much built the same. He brought me a complete outfit of his own clothes. While I was dressing he called a central credit card number and reported all my cards stolen.

He laughed. "They have probably charged a trillion dollars by now."

"That's not possible. I only have two cards and the max on each one is $5000.00."

"That's a relief," Tom said. "Listen, I've rescheduled the meetings for two weeks down the pike. You rest up and you can go home whenever."

"I think I'll hang in here until my regular departure time. The airlines charge a fortune to change flights," I said. All I could think of was that Mac would be back and maybe we could spend more time together than the usual one night stand. I figured I might as well make something positive out of a bad situation.

As he was leaving, Tom suddenly stopped and said, "Shit, I almost forgot. Here's a company cell phone so we can reach you. The number is on the tape on the back. After you memorize it, you can rip off the tape.

After Tom left, I took stock of my situation. I had no money and the credit card number on file with the hotel had been cancelled by Tom. I wasn't sure what I was to do so I called my home office. When I spoke to my boss he was more than sympathetic. He said he would call the front desk and give them a corporate card number which I could use at the hotel. There were restaurants and shops in the hotel so I could buy some clothes. But I would need money, so I asked the hotel to advance me some on the corporate card. I was all set.

I went to a clothing shop in the lobby and bought some additional underwear, socks, a tee shirt and slacks. There were no shoe stores on the premises, and Tom's shoes pinched a bit, but I could get by. I was just entering the elevator when Mac scooted in behind me. We nodded at each other, but said nothing.

As soon as we entered my room, I double locked the door and we embraced warmly. Mac grabbed my package and I asked if he could stay.

"Yes," he said. "I'm off until the day after tomorrow. Damn, I can't leave you alone for a minute. The one night I'm not at the bar, you fuck yourself up royally."

I answered that nasty remark by saying, "How about trusting me with your cell phone number, so I can call you in advance next time? My next trip will be in two weeks by the way."

"I trust you, baby," Mac said. He didn't have his note book with him, so he went over to the telephone table, wrote his number on a pad and handed the slip to me. "Wanna fuck before dinner?" he asked.

"What a dumb question," I answered. We were undressed, in bed, and wrapped up in each other's arms in seconds. I could feel his hard on pressing against me, and I began to shiver. Nobody, male or female, ever made me feel like Mac does. I was too hot for preliminaries and I dove right down on him. I gently took his balls in my hand and guided his beautiful uncut, eight inch cock into my mouth. Mac began to buck and moan and he shot his load so fast, I was frankly disappointed.

"Sorry," he apologized. I haven't had sex since your last visit. I haven't even whacked off. I wanted to save it for you. I'll give you more to suck on in a little while, but now let me do you."

I lay down on my back and Mac went to work. I had cum in one of the twin's mouths not too long ago, and I knew I would take longer to cum than he did. I wanted to concentrate on the great blow job he was giving me, but all I could think of were his last words. *I wanted to save it for you.* Those are the words of a man in love. When the realization that he loved me sunk in, I was overwhelmed. I realized that I loved him too. I wanted to be with him, but I could never leave my wife, and furthermore, we lived almost 500 miles apart. How much more fucked up could my life get? Thinking back on my life, I should have known that you can't live a lie forever. I should have been honest with the world and with myself.

I didn't have much more time to think about that, because Mac's magic was beginning to work. I could feel my orgasm building. Even without drugs I could tell that it was going to be a humdinger. I was right. There was no mess. Mac swallowed all my cum as I had done with him.

We lay side by side fondling each other. There was so much I wanted to say to him, but I was afraid. We were silent for a long time, and finally Mac said, "After dinner will you please fuck me?"

"Only if you do as much for me," I answered. I completely ignored my sore ass.

"Deal," he muttered as he began to nibble on my ear. I could bear it no longer and I began to cry.

"What's wrong, babe?" he asked. "Did I do something to hurt you?"

I decided to let it all out. I took a deep breath, and looked him straight in the eye. "You did nothing wrong at all," I said. "I'm the one who is all fucked up."

"What are you talking about?" he asked.

I stroked his cheek and leaned over to him so that I could whisper in his ear. "I'm madly in love with you, and that places me in an impossible situation. It's a dilemma. I don't know if I can ever resolve it."

I wasn't sure what kind of reaction to expect so when Mac began to cry all I could do was to hold him closer to comfort him. After a long while he mumbled into my chest, "I love you more, and I appreciate your dilemma. I don't want to be the cause of breaking up your marriage, but we have to find a way out. I want to be with you and it doesn't seem to be in the cards."

"We have all night and all day tomorrow to love each other and talk about this situation. My plane leaves at 5 PM. Maybe we can come up with a solution," I said optimistically.

"Yes," Mac said. "Let's get dressed and I'll take you to my favorite restaurant, *The Anchor Bar*, where Buffalo Chicken Wings were invented."

"Cool!" I said. We jumped out of bed and into the shower. Mac had asked me to fuck him after dinner, but as I washed his ass and inserted a couple of fingers, my erect, soapy cock somehow began to enter him, and he begged me to go deeper. As I had yet another orgasm up Mac's luscious ass, I began to laugh.

"What's so funny?" Mac asked.

"I just realized. I fucked a cop and I don't even know his name."

"My name is Cornelius MacNeal," he said. "If you laugh, you're a dead man. Everyone calls me Connie or Mac."

"Everyone calls me Wallie," I countered. Now that we had been formally introduced, we embraced each other. As we kissed passionately, the shower water fell on us, cleansing our bodies, and for the moment, erasing the burden of our impossible love.

We enjoyed our dinner but we did not linger. We didn't even go back to the gay bar where I was drugged. "Let's go to my place," Mac said. I want you to see where I live. On your next trip it would be great if you stayed with me. Your boss will love saving the hotel bill. You can say that you are staying with friends."

"That sounds wonderful," I said. "I always call home from my cell phone so Marsha would have no idea that I wasn't in a hotel. Shit," I suddenly yelled. "I need to call her." I took my new company phone out of my pocket.

My first call was to my cell phone provider to disconnect my old number. Unfortunately they told me that the thieves had already run up a sizeable bill. When I hung up, Mac told me to give him the bill when I received it. "Maybe we can trace the perps through the calls they made," he explained.

Then I called Marsha. I told her only that I had been robbed in my hotel room, but that I was perfectly all right and would be home as planned. I didn't tell her that the meetings had been cancelled. She asked me about the unfamiliar number I was calling from, and I explained that Tom had given me a company phone to use because mine had been stolen. She seemed satisfied.

Mac lived in a quiet suburb called Eggertsville. He had an upstairs apartment in a four plex. It was only a one bedroom, but it was spacious and tastefully decorated. Mac took my hand and led me into his bedroom. I looked at his king size bed and said jokingly, "It's your turn to fuck me, you know."

"It will be a pleasure."

Chapter Two

Mac and I made love all that night and into the next morning. Every so often we both dozed off, but we actually got very little sleep, and even less food. When we did sleep, we slept so entwined, it's a miracle of love that we slept at all.

Finally about one in the afternoon, we showered together, each of us taking delight in cleansing the other one's magnificent body. I hated to leave the shower but it was necessary. Mac made us bacon and eggs for breakfast in the afternoon. We delayed as long as possible, but finally Mac drove me back to the hotel. There I called Tom and told him that I would bring back his clothes on my next trip. I had to assure him that I was all right. I packed my suitcase with my meager belongings and called the bellboy.

While we waited, Mac and I stood there holding each other tightly, not wanting to let go. We only let go when there was a knock on the door. I tipped the bellboy for yesterday and today. He saw the two of us together, smiled and winked at me again. Without hesitation, I smiled and winked back. Before yesterday, I would have pretended not to notice.

I checked out and offered to take a cab to the airport, but Mac would have none of it. Several times on the way to the airport, we would reach over to each other and gently lay our hands on the other's package. Each time Mac did that, I got a terrible feeling of dread in the pit of my stomach. I wanted so badly to stay with him, but it was impossible. I didn't want to leave Buffalo, but I had to.

Mac stopped at the curb side check in and popped his trunk. Before we got out of the car, he squeezed my hand and I nearly cried out in agony. I wanted to yell, "Don't leave me," but after all, I was leaving him. I realized that I had never loved anyone like this; not my parents and not even Marsha. I was ashamed when I realized that I loved Mac more than my parents and my wife, but I consoled myself by trying to convince myself that it was a different kind of love. The fact of the matter is, it is a different kind of love.

I took my suitcase out of the trunk, and as the skycap was checking me into my flight, Mac jumped quickly back in his car. "Call me," I heard him say and I nodded my head. He was gone so fast, I hope he saw me nod.

I was the first person to sit in my row and I offered a silent prayer that nobody gabby would sit next to me. The flight to New York only took about an hour, give or take five minutes, but I wanted to be alone with my thoughts. My prayers were not answered, but in the end I was glad.

A young man put his carry on luggage in the overhead bin, and sat down next to me. He was too cute to believe. He looked like the all American boy next door in stories written around the turn of the twentieth century. He was about my height, blond curly hair, blue eyes, square chin and an amazing smile. He was wearing a University of Buffalo sweat shirt and too tight jeans which accentuated what he had to offer.

"Hi," he said as our eyes met. I smiled back at him as he settled in his seat and adjusted his seat belt. Suddenly I actually wanted to talk to this young man.

"Do you go to UB?" I asked as an ice breaker and pointing to his sweat shirt.

"Yes, I do," he said pleasantly. "Do you live in the Buffalo area or are you going home?"

"Home," I said. "Massapequa."

"Hey, I live in Oceanside. We're practically neighbors." He held out his hand. "My name is Jonathan."

"Shit," I said. "You're putting me on. My name is Jonathan also, but you can call me Wallie." We both laughed at that, just as my cell phone rang. We hadn't been asked yet to turn them off.

"Hi sexy," Mac's sultry voice said. "I miss you so much already, that when I left you, I drove right home so I could whack off and dream of you." I was very embarrassed. I'm sure that my seat mate could hear Mac very dimly. I was right. Jonathan was smiling at me.

"I'll call you when I get home," I said, "but I can't talk now. Believe me! I love you too."

"It's hard to be apart when you love someone, isn't it?" Jonathan asked, not expecting an answer. "That's why I'm taking a couple of days off from school. I haven't seen my sweetie since the semester began. One more day apart and I'll go crazy."

"You're a very handsome guy," I said. "I bet your girl friend is a stunner."

Jonathan laughed. "Oh yes, you're right. Let me show you a picture." He reached into his wallet and pulled out a picture which was slightly frayed at the edges. He handed it to me and I was shocked. There was Jonathan with his arm around an equally good looking guy. It seemed to me that the other man was maybe five years older than Jonathan. They were wearing skimpy bathing suits and I knew that the picture was taken at Jones Beach. I recognized the pier in the background.

"He's your lover?" I asked. Jonathan nodded.

"You make a beautiful couple and you don't know how I envy you."

"Why do you envy us?" he asked.

I don't know why, but I poured my heart out to this young man. As the plane lifted off the tarmac, I began my story including getting drugged and robbed. He sat in silence listening, and as we began our descent, he put his hand on mine. "I wish I could be wise enough to offer you a solution, but I can't," he said. "I know one thing for sure. If you and Mac are truly in love, soul mates even, love will find a way. I know it's corny, but I really believe that."

He reached into his wallet and gave me a card. "Please," he said, "when you get to Buffalo next time, call me. I'd love to meet Mac and have dinner with you both." I glanced at the card. His last name was Mallory.

"I promise," I said.

We walked together toward the security gate. I spotted Jonathan's lover before he did. He was younger than his picture would have me believe. He was probably the same age as Jonathan. "There's your young man," I said. Jonathan sprinted ahead and the two men fell into each other's arms. They kissed in full view of everyone. Most people pretended not to see, including Marsha who was watching them.

"Ahem," I said, and she turned to face me. She threw her arms around me and gave me a motherly peck on my cheek. *Ah Mac*, I mused, *I miss you're passion.*

"Did you see those two men kissing?" she asked. "Wasn't it disgusting?"

"I don't see anything disgusting about two people being in love, and displaying that love to the world. I think it's a beautiful thing."

Marsha didn't say anything, but her eyebrows went up as if to say, *I can't believe you said that."*

I made love to Marsha that night. I felt it was an obligation, and I knew that I would then be able to avoid it for about four more nights after that. As I fucked her, I imagined that I was fucking Mac and I got really hot. This prompted Marsha to say afterward, "You should be away more often. That was wonderful, darling."

The next day at the office, I turned in my temporary cell phone. I was told by the credit card companies that I would have my new credit cards in three business days. I left the office early to have time to purchase a new cell phone. The minute it was activated, I called Mac. He was at work and we couldn't talk, but he took my new number and thanked me. Then I called my wife, and gave her my new number. I lied to her. I told her I had to work late because I had been away so long. Instead of working, I went to a male porn theater and saw a couple of male films.

In the past, when I went to this theater, I would take my cock out and in a very short time someone would be sucking on it. This time, I stroked myself gently without removing it, and nobody approached me. The men on the screen kept turning into Mac and me, and I began to cry.

It was way past rush hour, when I boarded the Long Island Railroad train for home. I found a spot where there were few people sitting, and I called Mac. We talked all the way home, or I should say, we cried all the way home. After that I tried to call Mac at least once a day from my bathroom, and we jerked off together. I hated phone sex, but it brought me close to my lover, and so I gladly did it. I counted off every day until my next scheduled trip to Buffalo.

About four days before my departure, fate intervened. It was just after dinner, and I was watching Jeopardy! The phone rang, and Marsha answered it, listened a minute, and then put her hand over the speaker.

"It's a detective MacNeal from Buffalo, for you." For a moment I panicked, and my hand was shaking as I took the phone from her.

"Hello, detective," I tried to sound very business like.

"How are you Mr. Walters?" He didn't wait for an answer. "Good news. We have apprehended the twins who robbed you. Is there any chance you can get to Buffalo in the next day or two to identify them in a line-up?" My heart skipped a beat.

I'll need to check at my office tomorrow," I said. "Give me a number where I can reach you, and I'll let you know."

"Fair enough," Mac said, "and I have more good news. We recovered your watch and your wedding ring in their apartment. I guess they hadn't fenced it yet."

"That is good news, Detective. My wife will be particularly pleased about the ring. Thanks again and I'll call you tomorrow. Goodbye."

I was so excited about Mac's news, I began to hyperventilate, and I could hardly relate to her what Mac had told me. I couldn't sleep that night, wishing away the time until I could get to the office. I had my speech well rehearsed, and I didn't miss a beat as I told my boss about Mac's call.

"If I leave tonight, I'll take care of police business tomorrow, Thursday. That leaves only Friday and the weekend before my meetings start Monday morning, so I might as well stay in Buffalo. It will be cheaper than flying back and forth."

"Absolutely," my boss agreed, and I set my secretary to work making flight arrangements.

"What about the hotel?" she asked.

"Not this time," I said. "One robbery was enough for me. I'll be staying with a friend and saving the company a few bucks as well."

When everything was set, I went into my office, closed the door and called Mac. I gave him my arrival information. I was leaving on the last flight out tonight and would arrive in Buffalo a little after 11 PM. I was not returning until Tuesday night and I would be staying with him.

"I'll be at the airport with bells on," he said. I swear his voice cracked.

I left the office early and went home to pack. This was going to be a longer stay than usual and my suitcase was full and heavy and included Tom's clothes.

TOM!

Tom would want to come by the hotel and pick up his clothes. I had to think of something so as not to arouse his suspicion. Maybe I would tell him that a friend of mine from college had recently moved to the suburbs of Buffalo, and I was staying with him because I was still having nightmares about being drugged and robbed in the hotel. That sounded believable enough.

I would bring his clothes to the first meeting, or to the local office, whichever was most convenient. Yes, I thought, that should fly.

After a quick dinner Marsha drove me to the airport. A quick peck on the cheek and she was off. It occurred to me that she wasn't very sad to see me go. I also realized that we had not made love since the night I got home from Buffalo. Maybe she was sore about that. If she was angry, why didn't she make an attempt to initiate sex? I had never sensed anything wrong with our marriage, but at that moment, I began to suspect that Marsha wasn't the happy housewife I thought she was. I vowed to talk to her about it when I returned. If something was wrong I wanted to make it right. I did not want to be unfair to Marsha or neglect her own sexual needs.

Marsha has an MS in Clinical Psychology. She gave up her career when she married me. I begged her not to do it, so she couldn't be angry at me for that. She wanted to stay at home and have a baby, but we had not been successful, even though several doctors could find nothing wrong with either of us.

The hell with all that. In about two hours, I'd be in Mac's arms. I could already smell his distinct aroma and taste his cock. I could even imagine how he felt inside my ass. I was getting hard and tried to think of something else.

The skycap took my bag and handed me my claim check and boarding pass. After I went through security, I still had an hour until departure, so I headed for the bar. A beer or two would help the time pass more quickly. Needless to say, each minute was an hour to me.

Once we were airborne, the flight crew dimmed the cabin lights. I tried to doze but I was too excited. I kept creating images in my head of making love to Mac. If I had to go to the bathroom, I would not have been able to stand up. My hard on was ripping at my trousers.

I had flown enough to know when we were beginning our decent. I was aware of it long before the captain informed us. I grew even more excited, if that was possible. I would love to greet Mac just as Jonathan Mallory had greeted his lover, but Mac was a cop. I needed to be more discreet.

I had been fortunate enough to obtain a seat up front so I got off the plane rather quickly. I ran with abandon toward the security gate. The moment I saw Mac, I broke out into a sweat. He was holding his arms open and I jumped into them. We hugged so tightly, we could not get any closer, but we refrained from kissing. We started toward baggage claim chattering away like school girls. I wanted to grab his hand, but held myself back. I felt like an addict trying to resist his addiction.

It wasn't until we were in Mac's car that we finally kissed. Oh what a kiss. Our tongues reached deep into each other's mouths. I thought I might die of asphyxiation and determined that it was a great way to go. Each time one of us came up for air and could talk a little, all we could say was, "I love you."

When we got home, I didn't bother to unpack. We undressed and headed right for Mac's bed. We made love for hours until Mac said, "My God, it's 4AM. We have to get some sleep. I'll be taking you to the station in five hours.

Neither of us could sleep well so we rose early and showered together. I even had time to unpack and hang up my clothes. Tom's suit was in a plastic carrier bag. His other clothes were in my suitcase. I transferred them to a plastic bag.

I said to Mac, "After the lineup, I'll take Tom's clothes to my local office. Where would be a good place to pick me up after you leave work?"

"I'll call when I leave the station. Why don't you meet me at The Anchor Bar? But what will you do in the interim?"

"I'll hang around the office and prepare for my meeting on Monday. Don't worry about me," I said.

I had only seen lineups in the movies so I didn't know what to expect. I stood behind a one way glass. Mac stood next to me, which relieved some of my anxiety. "Here they come," Mac said.

Four sets of twins marched across the stage. They were all young and very good looking, but only Ryan and Sean looked younger than the legal fucking age. I pointed them out immediately.

"Good," Mac said. "I know it will be a financial burden and difficult on your work schedule, but you will have to come back to Buffalo for the trial if they plead not guilty. In fact, you may have to come several times."

"I'll do what I have to do, Detective," I said and held out my hand to Mac, who shook it with a gleam in his eye. "I'll be in Buffalo until Tuesday night," I said. "Here's my business card. It has the New York numbers where you can reach me after I leave Buffalo. If you give me a pencil I'll write my cell phone number on the card, and you can reach me anytime here in Buffalo. I congratulated myself on my Academy Award performance.

"Thank you," Mac said. "We'll have no trouble reaching you. Can I drop you off anywhere?" he asked.

"My local office would be nice," I said. It's in The Liberty Bank Building."

"Not a problem," Mac said. "Just follow me to the desk clerk and I'll give you your property. After that we'll go to my car."

We met that night at The Anchor Bar as planned, but this evening we did not rush. Mac had arranged to take a personal day off on Friday so we had the whole weekend to be together. That was great for both of us because we couldn't get enough of each other. We had a nice dinner, but since Mac was our designated driver, he only had one Miller Lite, followed by one O'Doul's. I'm not a big drinker and I sipped two Millers for a couple of hours. We so enjoyed being together, that we didn't even realize how much time had passed.

"Let's go," Mac said. It sounded almost like a plea. In the car he bravely asked me if my wife suspected anything about my double life.

"I would have said, 'absolutely not' a couple of days ago, but she was rather cool at the airport when she said goodbye to me. I'm not certain anymore."

"Well," Mac said, "unless you called her from your office, you haven't called her once since you arrived."

"Shit," I said and I whipped out my cell phone. I heard four rings and then the answering machine picked up. I left Marsha a message telling her briefly that I had identified the guys who robbed me and had my watch and ring back. I spent the afternoon at the office and now was on my way to bed after dinner. I artfully neglected to say where that bed was. I told her I loved her and missed her and hung up.

"Wouldn't it be great," Mac said, "if neither of us had to tell lies any more?"

"Amen," I said. Then for the first time I told Mac about Jonathan Mallory and the great trip I had on the way home from Buffalo, and how wonderful it was that he could express his love openly.

"I promised to have dinner with him when I got here. He's dying to meet you. How about tomorrow evening? If you know a nice place near the campus, I'll call him."

"Get him on the phone and then hand the phone to me. I'll tell him where and when to meet us."

Jonathan answered on the second ring. He sounded delighted to hear from me. I explained briefly why I was back in Buffalo prematurely. I asked if he was free for dinner with us tomorrow evening and he said he was.

"Hold on a sec," I said and handed the phone to Mac. They made up to meet at seven the next evening, at a place, and on a street, that I had never heard of. When he got off the phone, Mac handed it to me.

"Where are we going?" I asked.

"To a nice little Italian restaurant right off campus. It's gay owned and most of the clientele are usually gay. It's a comfortable place for us to be, and the food is great."

"I can't wait to sample the cuisine," I said, "and I can't wait for you to meet young Jonathan."

"And I can't wait to fuck you tonight, and tomorrow and tomorrow night and forever after," Mac said to me as he grabbed my cock.

A Boner Book

Chapter Three

Mac was lying on top of me. His well lubed cock was moving playfully up and down my crack. He did this for awhile and then he positioned the head at my opening and started his entry. He was about half way in when my cell phone rang. He started to pull out, but I yelled at him to please continue. As he did, I reached for my phone. It was less than an arm's length away on the night table.

"Keep fucking me," I ordered. "This should be a hoot."

"Hello!"

"Where the hell are you? Are you shacking up with some floozie?" Marsha's voice!! I panicked and pushed Mac off of me.

"Calm down," I said. "I'm in Buffalo.

"I'm in Buffalo too," she said. "I'm at the Sheraton and you haven't even checked in. I wanted to surprise you and spend the weekend with you. I thought we had something special between us. Why are you cheating on me?"

"Honey, honey, honey, I'm not cheating. Please let me explain. Ever since I was robbed, I have developed a great fear of hotels. I'm afraid to go into them. I've started therapy," I lied. "When I told Detective MacNeal about it, he generously said that I could use his spare bedroom. He wouldn't even let me rent a car, and has been chauffeuring me around until we both go back to work on Monday." I never lied to Marsha before, and I felt so guilty. She didn't say a word and I was really worried.

"Please darling, get us a room, and I'll be there as soon as possible. I promise you, we'll have a great weekend." Still silence.

I was about to plead for Marsha to speak to me, when she said, "Oh my poor darling. Why didn't you tell me how traumatic the robbery was for you? You led me to believe it was nothing at all. Yes, I'll get a room. Just hurry over. I'll see you shortly."

"I guess you heard," I said to Mac. "I am so sorry, my love. I never thought she would do something like this."

"I understand," Mac said, "but I don't like it." He started to cry. "It's not going to work between us. Maybe we shouldn't see each other again."

"Oh God," I said. "Please don't say that. Give me some time. I swear I'll work it out. Just don't give up on me. I love you so much."

We were pretty quiet in the car driving down town until I said something at last. "Please meet Jonathan tomorrow and tell him what happened, and how sorry I am."

"Yes, of course, I will."

I described Jonathan to Mac, and again we were silent. He dropped me off in front of the hotel and when I went to kiss him goodbye, he turned his head away. I was devastated. I wanted to cry, but tried not to. After all, I had to face Marsha in a few minutes.

"She's leaving Sunday night," I said. "Please see me after her plane leaves and again on Monday evening. We'll have two nights together. I'm not leaving until late Tuesday evening." Mac remained silent. I pleaded once again. "Please Mac. I beg you."

He turned to me and kissed me. "What can I do? I'm hopelessly in love with you too. Of course, I'll see you. Call me as soon as she leaves."

I hopped out of the car, feeling much better, and Mac drove off. The desk clerk gave me a key to the room Marsha had obtained and I hurried upstairs, hoping to minimize the rift between us. I let myself in and Marsha ran sobbing to me. I dropped my suitcase where I was standing, and I embraced her and tried to soothe her.

"Please." I begged," don't cry.

"Oh my darling," she sobbed. "When I suspected you of cheating, I wanted to kill myself. I can't bear the thought of a life without you. If anything ever happened to you, I think I would end my own life." That was not what I needed to hear.

"Don't talk that way," I said. "Nothing is going to happen to me and I'm never going to leave you."

"Well," Marsha said, "maybe something will. No wonder you were robbed in a hotel room. When you came in, you didn't double lock the door." I started to laugh.

"Touché," I said and ran to the door.

"Make love to me," Marsha said seductively.

I started to undress, all the while staring at Marsha. I willed her image to turn into Mac. I envisaged what Mac and I were doing when she called me. I was willing myself into arousal, and it was working. I shut the lights and climbed into bed with my eyes closed. I really made myself believe that Mac was in bed with me, and when Marsha/Mac's hand caressed my cock, it stiffened to my delight, and certainly to Marsha's.

After a tourist has viewed Niagara Falls from the Canadian side, Buffalo is not much of a tourist town, so we spent most of the weekend in bed. I was able to function well enough, and although I imagined myself fucking Mac instead of Marsha, I truly missed his cock up my ass. I couldn't wait for Marsha to go home, and even though I had to work Monday and most of Tuesday, I would have Sunday and Monday nights with Mac. I swore to tell him how much I missed and loved him.

After he left me on Thursday evening, Mac drove right home. He cried most of the way, bemoaning our impossible situation. When he got home, he went straight to bed. He wanted to finish what we had started earlier that evening. He stroked his cock repeatedly, but he was so upset, he couldn't cum, even with a familiar enough hand job.

He had no reason to get up on Friday morning and so he stayed in bed until late afternoon. He didn't eat a thing. Finally late in the afternoon, he got out of bed and went to the bathroom. He relieved himself, showered and shaved. He knew he was going to meet a handsome young stud that evening so he put on lots of after shave lotion. He wanted to dress in a sexy tank top, but it was late fall, almost winter, and Buffalo was cold and blustery. Almost every day now, snow flurries were in the air. Pretty soon, the first big snow fall would descend on the city, coming in from Lake Erie, and Buffalo would be blanketed in a white mantle.

He put on a flannel shirt over a white t-shirt, and heavy denim jeans. He wore no underwear. He never did, no matter how cold it got. He finished with crew socks and work boots, appropriate for the cold weather. He took a good look at himself in the mirror. He liked what he saw. He was thirty-five, almost three years older than I, but the face staring back at him looked even younger than mine. Jonathan was a college freshman, so he was probably eighteen or at most nineteen. He was pleased that he could probably pass as Jonathan's contemporary or maybe his slightly older brother.

Just before seven, Mac walked into Mario's restaurant. As he was removing his fleece lined jacket, a friendly voice said, "Detective Mac, how nice to see you. It's been too long."

"Mario," Mac said, and embraced the man who greeted him. "You are so right. It has been too long." He let Mario go and said, "I'm supposed to meet a young student here named Jonathan. Would he be here yet?"

"I think you mean that *hottie* at the corner table, but he asked us to set it for three."

"Yes, I know. You can remove one setting. My other friend can't make it." Mac and Mario walked over to the table together and Mario whispered into Mac's ear, "Lucky you."

Mac introduced himself to Jonathan. They shook hands and Jonathan said, "I'm Jonathan Mallory." As Mario removed the extra setting, Mac could see the confused look on Jonathan's face.

"I'll explain as soon as we've ordered our wine," he said.

When the wine came, they toasted themselves and the missing Wallie. "Well?" Jonathan asked.

Mac could not have been blunter. "I was just inserting my cock into Wallie's ass, when his cell phone rang." He was pleased to notice that Jonathan did not seem to mind his bluntness at all. "It was his wife. She had come to Buffalo to surprise him and to spend the weekend together."

"Bummer," Jonathan interjected.

"Needless to say, that put an end to the fantastic weekend of sex that we had planned. But I'm pleased to say that although I am very disappointed, I am still in love with the guy, and we will have Sunday and Monday nights together. She leaves late on Sunday and Wallie will call me when the coast is clear.

"Now that you are all filled in, and Wallie has told you all about me, I want to hear all about you and your boyfriend. What's his name, what's he do etc?"

Jonathan took a deep breath and began. "To begin with, his name is Jake McLean and everybody calls him Mac. So we are left with two Jonathan's, but one is a Wallie, and two Mac's, but I always call him Jake so there will be no confusion. I think it's a hell of a coincidence that the four of us share two names.

"Jake transferred into my high school when we were both freshman. His dad was originally from Oceanside, but he moved to Milwaukee when he married Jake's mother, who was born there. He never made a lot of friends in Milwaukee, and when Jake's mother died, his father renewed his friendship with an old high school sweetheart back home. She was recently divorced. He and Jake moved back to New York, and Jake's father married his old girlfriend. When he came back, he opened a delicatessen in Oceanside. The deli has been very successful and that's what separated us. But I am skipping too far ahead.

"From the minute I met Jake, we became best friends. We were inseparable, and by the time we were graduating high school, we knew that we were soul mates, and we wanted to share our lives.

"Our first obstacle hit us when I was applying to SUNY Buffalo. Jake's father wouldn't let him go. He said that he was getting older and needed Jake to run the store, which would be his someday anyway. Jake and I had long talks about it. We concluded that I was college material and he wasn't. The truth of the matter is that Jake really wants the store, so off I went to college and we are left with raging hardons and occasional phone sex. That's about it," he said. "Any questions?"

"Well, I can feel for you. Wallie and I have phone sex often, but we both hate it. We long for each other so desperately and we can't be together. I am always so horny, I have trouble hiding the bulge in my pants."

Jonathan started to laugh. "Sometimes in class, I completely lose track of what the prof is saying, and I day dream about fucking Jake or about him fucking me. When the bell rings, it would be a major university scandal if I stood up."

That got them both laughing and giggling hysterically, and some of the restaurant customers turned to see what was going on.

Mac said, "You know all this talk has turned me on. I've got an erection right now."

"So have I," Jonathan told Mac. I can't wait to get back to the dorm and jerk off under the sheets."

"Why under the sheets?" Mac asked.

"Well, I can't do it in the bathroom. It's too public. My room mate is straight, and he's getting plenty of pussy, so he doesn't have to jerk off. I do it surreptitiously under the sheets even if he isn't there. I don't want him walking in on me and making jokes about my not getting any."

"Last night, after I left Wallie, I was very horny from our interrupted sex," Mac confided. "I tried to whack off, but I was so upset, I couldn't make it. Maybe I'll be luckier tonight."

"All you need is a little stimulation," Jonathan advised.

"You're probably right," Mac said, "and you have given me an idea. Why jerk off in fear of getting caught? Come home with me, and we can both do it openly and freely while dreaming of our lovers. It wouldn't mean anything, if we helped each other along either. And I don't think either of them would mind, knowing we were pretending we were with them. Besides, I know that Wallie is fucking his wife's brains out. Why shouldn't I get some too?"

"I don't know," Jonathan said. "I've never cheated on Jake. He's the only guy I have ever been with."

"That's the point. It wouldn't be cheating. All we would be doing is getting our horny rocks off. Besides if you have never been with another guy, I might be able to give you some pointers that will blow Jake's mind."

"That did it. You just sold me," Jonathan said with a happy grin.

"How did you get here?" Mac asked Jonathan.

"I walked from my dorm."

"Good," Mac said. "I'll drive." When they finished eating, he paid the bill, hugged Mario good night and left with Jonathan.

When they arrived at Mac's apartment, he was pleased to see that Jonathan was not the least bit nervous. Mac does not need to hide his sexuality, and there are pictures of male nudes all over the apartment. Jonathan got busy looking at each one while Mac poured them glasses of wine. They both sat on the sofa, their thighs touching. Mac reached over and laid his hand on Jonathan's package. Jonathan did not flinch, but he put his glass down, leaned over and started to kiss Mac. Mac put his glass down also. They embraced and began to kiss in earnest. Their tongues clashed and their hands began to explore all the possibilities.

Mac pulled away. "Are you sure?" he asked. "We were just going to whack each other off, but we are starting to act like two lovers."

"I'm sure," Jonathan said. "You don't know how badly I need this, but I must warn you that I fully intend to tell Jake all about this. We love each other and I know he'll understand."

"And I intend to tell Wallie. The worst thing that two lovers can do is hold secrets between them." Mac took Jonathan's hand and led him to the bedroom. There, they began to undress each other. When they were naked they just stood and admired each other. Both were uncut, and Mac was about an inch longer than Jonathan. The girth of their cocks was about the same.

"I like what I see," Jonathan exclaimed.

"Me too," Mac said. "Now get into bed and let me do all the work. I'm going to give you a sample of grown up, man sex."

"That suits me fine," Jonathan said. "I didn't automatically become a man on my eighteenth birthday." He climbed into bed and lay flat on his back. Mac climbed in also, lay down on top of him, and pushed his tongue down Jonathan's throat. After a long while, Mac began his sensuous trip around the world. He tongued up and down Jonathan's body for almost two hours. He was in no hurry. The next day was Saturday and neither had to go anywhere at all. They could stay in bed all day if they wanted to.

First Mac explored Jonathan's eyebrows and eyelashes, licking them softly. Then his tongue found Jonathan's ears and it darted in and out. He began to stroke Jonathan's throat with the tip of his tongue as Jonathan mewled softly. Mac worked downward, biting and suckling Jonathan's nipples, his belly button, and his pubic area. He was very careful not to touch Jonathan's cock or his balls, but he licked at the delicate vein between the bottom of the balls and the beginning of the crack. That nearly drove Jonathan crazy. His whole body was bucking as if he were riding an untamed bronco.

Mac started down the inside of both thighs and kissed each of Jonathan's ten toes, fondling them in his mouth. Finally, he rolled Jonathan over and he lay fully on top of him. His tongue started to nibble the back of Jonathan's neck and then he worked his way down Jonathan's back. When Mac reached Jonathan's southern cheeks, he spread them and began to lick up and down Jonathan's crack.

Jonathan began to invoke the name of the almighty. "Oh God," he cried over and over. He and Jake had never done this. Mac's tongue finally lingered at Jonathan's man cunt and he started to push into the hole. At this point Jonathan didn't care who could hear, he screamed out in ecstatic pleasure. When his screaming reached fever pitch, Mac rolled him over and took him at last. Mac's mouth fully enveloped Jonathan's cock, which tickled the back of Mac's throat. His tongue expertly licked up and down the underside of Jonathan's shaft. Jonathan could only moan and push his cock further into Mac's mouth. His balls began to shrink and Mac stopped sucking immediately.

"Why did you stop?" Jonathan screamed. "I need so badly to cum."

"You'll see," Mac said. He got out of bed and reached into his night table. He took out a condom and rolled it down Jonathan's rod. Then he extracted some lube from a tube and generously greased the condom. He put some more lube on his forefinger and lubed his own ass until it was glistening. He then straddled Jonathan. He reached under and took Jonathan's slimy cock into his own slimy hand and positioned it at his ass hole. He sat down on the messy cock and slowly lowered himself on it until all of it was inside of him.

"How does that feel?" he asked Jonathan.

"You've killed me with sex, and I've gone to heaven," Jonathan answered.

Mac began to move up and down on Jonathan's cock. On the up stroke, Jonathan brushed Mac's prostate, and on the down stroke, he nearly crushed it. The college boy screamed, "I love what you are doing. Please don't stop." With that, he started stroking down when Mac stroked up, and up when Mac stroked down. Mac's prostate was rebelling at the friction and he knew he was going to cum before Jonathan.

With a loud scream, Mac came, shooting cum up Jonathan's chest and chin and even reaching his mouth. Jonathan licked hungrily at Mac's semen. When he came, Mac's ass contracted and Jonathan yelled, "It's my turn." He came ferociously, bucking and screaming. The condom could not contain all of his jism and it started to run out the top, and down his ass.

Eventually they both calmed down. Jonathan's cock fell out of Mac's ass, leaving the condom inside. Mac pulled it out and ran to the bathroom where he dropped it down the toilet.

"Did you learn something?" Mac asked climbing back into bed.

"Absolutely! I learned how to make love. Up until now, we were having sex and it was very mechanical. I can't wait to pass this on to Jake."

"I promise you. It will be better with Jake, because you two have an emotional tie. Love always adds to the mix. Tomorrow morning, after we have rested, you can practice on me."

They lay side by side, holding hands. Just as they were falling asleep, the phone rang. Mac looked at the luminous dial on the clock on his dresser. "My God, it's 3 AM. Who the hell can this be?" He picked up the phone.

"Hello," he said.

"My darling," I said in a whispered voice. "I am so sorry about all this. I fucked her until I had no more to give, and she is finally sound asleep. God, I miss you. I want you so badly."

"Yes, honey. I love you too. But don't let her hear you. Please hang up and go to sleep."

"Did you meet Jonathan Mallory?" I asked.

"Yes. He's lying here, right beside me."

Chapter Four

"What did you say?" I asked.

Mac repeated, "He's lying here, right beside me. Would you like to say hello?" I was so flabbergasted I actually said that I'd like to speak to Jonathan.

Mac put him on, and I heard him say, "Now Wallie, just relax. Mac is all yours. He was just giving me lessons to use on my guy. I must admit it was a wonderful lesson, and I can't wait to try it on Jake."

"Jonathan," I said, "I have screwed up my life to the nth degree. Don't ever be afraid to be who you are. Every chance you get, just tell your man how much you love him. You can't tell it to him enough. I'm sorry I didn't get to see you. Maybe we can get together Sunday or Monday evening. Work it out with Mac. Now please put him back on."

After a couple of seconds, Mac said, "Hi guy. I love you, you know."

"I love you too. I sure wish I could have shared Jonathan with you. It's been a long time since I have enjoyed college meat."

"We're not finished yet. We have all day tomorrow for more lessons."

"I can't tell you how jealous I am. Give him one for me," I told Mac. "I've really got to go now. I just needed to know that *we* are all right."

"We'll be all right forever, no matter what. Just keep fucking Marsha and I'll keep on instructing Jonathan."

"You have a better deal," I said, but hopefully someday I'll be able to share him with you, and live a life that will make me happy. Goodnight, sweetheart."

Finally, the ordeal was over. At 4 PM on Sunday, I put Marsha in a cab and sent her to the airport. It had been threatening to snow all day and I silently prayed that the plane would take off and get her home on time. It never did snow. I did not check out of the hotel for obvious reasons. I found a cab and went straight to Mac's place. I was greeted with hugs and kisses by both Mac and Jonathan. I was in heaven and walking on clouds.

The two men were naked when they let me in and the three of us undressed me rather quickly. "Why don't you show Wallie some of the techniques I taught you, Jonathan? Show him what a good teacher I am."

They took me into the bedroom and put me in the bed flat on my back. The two of them began to explore my body with their tongues, but it was Jonathan who ultimately went down on me. Mac taught him well. His tongue was blowing my mind, and I blew my cock into the first decent orgasm I had in days.

After that, I begged each of them to fuck me. It felt so good to have a solid cock up my ass again and I began to cry.

What's wrong baby?" Mac asked.

"Nothing, my darling. It's just that I'm so fucking happy.

Then I remembered Marsha. I took out my cell phone and called her. She told me that the weather was bad and she had a bumpy ride. She had just arrived home, albeit, a couple of hours late. I said, "Thank God. I'm so glad you are safe. I'll stay in touch, baby. Have a good night."

"I'll try," she answered me, and we hung up.

The three of us got up exceptionally early the next morning, and only Mac showered. He drove Jonathan back to his dorm where he could shower. Then he dropped me at my hotel. He told me that he would pick me up after work, but I said that I couldn't wait that long and that I would take a cab to his apartment, as I had done the night before. When I got into my room, I showered, changed clothes and headed for the first of two meetings regarding the marketing of the new breakfast cereal.

This time the gods were good to me. The snow did not come until about 4 PM, just as I was finishing my first meeting on Monday. I returned to the hotel and threw a few necessities into my carry on bag including my cell phone charger. I had no intention of returning to the hotel until Tuesday to check out.

It was snowing lightly at first, and I had no trouble getting a cab to Mac's apartment. He told me where I could find a key. I let myself in and waited for his arrival. I was so excited, I began to hyperventilate, and I had to start taking deep breaths.

At about 6 PM, Mac came home. He knocked on the door, which I thought was strange, but when I opened it up, I could see why. His arms were full of bags of groceries. After he put the bags on the kitchen counter he went back to his car for even more groceries.

"What's cooking?" I asked.

"Nothing yet, but there's a good chance we'll be snowbound for a few days. Look out the window." The blinds were closed. I opened them up. It was dark already, but I could see by the lights in the parking lot that it was snowing so hard, it was practically a white out. Mac's parking space was underneath a light and I could see that his car already had a good coating of snow.

"I called Jonathan to tell him that it would be too dangerous for me to pick him up tonight," Mac said with a grin, "so baby, it's just you and me." He smiled his heart melting smile, and we fell into each other's arms.

"Let's put the groceries away, and we'll figure out what to eat tonight. If we do get snowbound, and wouldn't that be great, we will certainly eat well," Mac said, with the pride of a man who has planned ahead. I actually don't know what we ate for dinner. We never really had a meal when it was supposed to be eaten. We just kept making love, and when we needed to rest, we ate whatever was handy. This went on far into the night until we fell asleep in each other's arms, fondling our over worked cocks.

I optimistically set the alarm clock the evening before for a 7 AM wake up. When I went to the window at 7, it was still dark and if it is possible, it was snowing harder. Mac's car was nowhere to be seen. Mac was still sleeping and snoring lightly. I waited until 7:30 to call Tom.

"Go back to sleep," he told me. There will be no meeting today. Anyway, we accomplished enough yesterday that we don't need any more meetings this round. I tried to reach you at the hotel, but you didn't answer. Were you in the shower?"

If I was going to be here for a few days I decided to tell Tom the truth. "I'm not at the hotel. I had dinner with a friend last night, and now I'm stuck in HIS apartment. You can always reach me on my cell phone.

"I didn't know you had friends in Buffalo, besides me, of course," Tom said.

"I don't, but it's the detective who found the twins who robbed me. We've just somehow become friends thanks to those two low lives."

That's great," Tom said. "Well, enjoy the snow, and stay in touch."

Tom is a bachelor so imagine my shock, when just as we were hanging up, I distinctly heard a very deep, male voice in the background, ask Tom, "Who were you talking to honey?"

My mind began to work overtime. Tom himself thought I was his only friend in Buffalo. Yet whenever I was here, he never asked me to have dinner with him or to go out somewhere with him. Could it be possible that Tom is gay, and he wanted to hide the fact from me? I didn't know for sure, but I was determined to find out at the first opportunity.

Mac was still sleeping, so I went to his computer, and I googled Tom Baker of Buffalo, NY. I was immediately rewarded with his age, addresses, and telephone numbers for his last three residences, all in Buffalo. Also listed as residing at his last two residences, was a Dominick Gallini. No other information was given about Dominick. It still wasn't proof positive.

I turned on the TV. The airport was closed, and officials were uncertain as to when it would reopen. Crews were working hard to clear the fields but the snow was falling faster than they could dig out. The city was at a standstill. People with flights out, were urged to stay in touch with their airlines. I tried to call them, but all I got was a busy signal. I was hungry but I didn't want to eat breakfast alone, so I brushed my teeth (with Mac's toothbrush) and crawled back into bed with him.

He was lying on his side and I nested against him. My cock was soft, and I crushed it against his crack. He purred slightly as if to let me know that he was aware of my presence and he liked it. In just a few minutes, I fell asleep again. We didn't sleep too much longer. We had showered after our last sexual encounter just a few short hours ago, so we didn't bother to do so again. Mac brushed his teeth and when he was finished, he kissed me, and he said to me. "You used my toothbrush, didn't you?"

"How did you know?"

"Foolish man. I'm a detective." He threw a bathrobe at me and put one on himself. We went into the kitchen and made ourselves pancakes and coffee. At the kitchen table, Mac remarked that he missed the morning paper.

Of course, it was not delivered that morning. That's when I suddenly lost it and let loose a torrent of tears.

Concerned, Mac ran over, put his arms around me and asked me what was wrong.

"You're a detective. You tell me." I said sarcastically.

Mac accepted the challenge. "Well, you are being overwhelmed by all this gay domesticity. This is the way you would like to spend the rest of your life. Knowing that you can't, has saddened you, and made you cry. For what it's worth, this is exactly how I would like to spend the rest of my life; with you. I love you so much it hurts."

We held each other tightly, both of us sobbing.

"Look," I said, "this snowstorm is a little gift from God. Let's be grateful and make the most of it." Mac nodded and returned to his seat at the table. Just then the phone rang. It was Jonathan lamenting the fact that he had not come to us before the storm started. All his classes were cancelled, and he had studied as much as he could. He said that he called Jake at the store. They spoke for a few minutes but Jake could not talk long. After we assured him that we both loved him, he finally hung up. The poor boy sounded so lonely.

After we cleaned up the breakfast dishes, we sat together on the couch, holding hands and watching TV. We learned that the storm was not expected to let up until early the next morning, and city officials did not expect services to be restored for at least forty-eight hours after that. At least two people were happy and I couldn't help wondering how many other couples in love were happy to be stranded together also. That put me in mind of Tom and Dominick. I told Mac what had happened when I called and about my Google results.

Mac had never actually met Tom, so I couldn't rely on any gaydar he might possess. We discussed how we might do a little detective work. Mac had several ideas. First, he went to his computer and with his special access code he was able to get into his office computer. He looked up Dominick Gallini.

Dominick was clean as a whistle except for one little incident fifteen years ago. Dominick was cruising in a park well known for this activity. A teen ager approached him, and when Dominick allowed the boy to touch him, he was immediately arrested by the undercover cop, who just happened to look young enough to pass as a teenager. At the police station Dominick pointed out that the cop had approached him, that the cop was of legal age, and he had never touched the young man. They let him go with some very stern warnings. That was the only thing Mac could turn up.

"Well," Mac said, "we know he's gay, he lives with Tom, and he calls Tom, Honey. Is that enough detective work for you."

"Sure," I said. "But I want Tom to know that we are brothers. I shouldn't do it, but I feel a need to come out to him. What do you think?"

"You're friends and co-workers. If you can rely on his discretion, I say do it. In my experience, the more you 'come out,' the easier it becomes each time you do after that."

I thought about it all morning, and determined that I would call Tom before the day was out, but I had no idea what I would say to him. Mac and I discussed it, and Mac felt that I should come right out and tell him that I was gay. If Tom was straight, it would be a test of his friendship. If he was gay, he would certainly come out to me. All I had to do was to be sure of his discretion relative to Marsha.

I waited until after dinner, and dialed Tom's number. A deeper, more mature sounding man said, "Hello," and I knew it was Dominic. I hesitated for a second and said something that took all of my courage,

"Hi, Dom. Is your partner home?"

"Sure he is," Dominick answered without missing a beat. "Where the hell can anyone go in weather like this anyway? I'll get him. Who shall I say is calling?"

"I'm an old friend and I want to surprise him so just say you don't know who is looking for him."

"As you like it!" Dom said and there was silence for a moment until I heard Tom say, "Hi, and which old friend are you?"

"Relax Tom, it's only me, Wallie," I said. "I'm looking forward to meeting your friend. Let's have dinner together the next time I'm in town or maybe before I leave."

The silence was deafening, as they say. I was prompted to say, "Tom, are you there? Were we cut off?"

Finally, Tom croaked, "Yes, I'm here Wallie. You know about me, don't you?"

"Yes Tommy, baby, I do."

"Have you told anyone? You won't tell anyone at work will you? How the hell did you find out?"

"Well, I'm obviously more astute than you are. How come you didn't figure out about me?" I asked.

More and more silence. Finally I heard, "But Wallie you're married."

"Yes, I'm married even though I've been gay all my life, and I am also counting on you not to out me, especially to Marsha."

"Never, I'd never do that. The guy you are snowbound with, is he really the detective on your case?"

"Yes, but I've known him for about two years. We met at Stoney's, the gay bar."

"I've been with Dom so long, we practically never go to bars any more. Otherwise we most certainly would have run into each other. Why are you coming out to me now?" Tom asked.

"Because, I want the whole world to know how much I love Mac, and how happy I am when I am with him. When I realized that you were gay, I knew I could trust you and I picked you to shout out to."

"Thanks for your trust in me, Wallie. You are a true friend. I can't wait for you to meet Dom, and I can't wait to meet Mac."

"Listen," I said, "as soon as the airport opens, I'll re-book for the following morning. I'll tell Marsha and the home office that it was the first available flight out. The four of us can meet for dinner the evening before my flight. How does that sound?"

"It sounds like a great plan. Wallie, I gotta say something before we hang up. Thank you for confiding in me. We've been friends a long time, and I've wanted to tell you about me and Dom a hundred times, but I didn't have the courage. Now that it's out, I don't feel like a mere friend any more. I feel like your brother. I love you man."

"I love you too," I said, as we both started to weep.

"We're keeping our eyes on the TV and we'll call as soon as we know when I can fly home and when we can have dinner together. Ciao, Tom."

I hung up and smiled broadly at Mac. "You were right," I said. "I have a brother now, and a brother-in-law, I guess. I've just started the nucleus of our gay family. I hope that we can also include Jake and Jonathan."

Mac smiled and gave me one hell of a bear hug. I could barely breathe. Just then the phone rang, and Mac picked it up. He had a short conversation and handed me the phone. "It's for you," he said.

"Wallie," I heard Tom say, "I got Mac's number off my phone log. I am so excited. We just can't hang up like that. You've got to tell me everything; when you knew you were gay; why you married; how you fell in love with Mac. I want to know everything."

Tom and I talked far into the evening. I told him everything I could about me; my youth; my school days; my stupid decision to try to live a straight life; my relationship with Mac; even my chance meeting with my gay son, Jonathan Mallory.

I learned that he and Dominick had been together for twelve years. Jonathan teaches Romance Languages at the University of Buffalo, and was in his twenty-fifth year there. My suspicion that he was a good deal older than Tom was true.

I went into the bedroom where Mac was waiting for me. He smiled and said, "I'm really happy for you, my love. Now how about I make you happy too?"

Chapter Five

It stopped snowing about four o'clock in the morning. We woke about three hours later to a bleak sky and frigid temperatures. Mac decided to make us oatmeal for breakfast. "This kind of weather calls for it," he announced. Of course, we were glued to the TV for word of the airport opening. It was almost impossible to get through to the airlines by telephone.

After breakfast, we showered and got right back into bed. We were all done out from constant love making, but we wrapped around each other, cuddled and fondled. This was better than any orgasm. This was a display of our love, an opportunity to exhibit total intimacy, and to say over and over again, "I love you." We squeezed our asses and crushed our limp dicks together, and once we actually got hard again, so we fucked each other. It took each of us a long time to cum, and we liked it that way.

About two o'clock in the afternoon, we heard the unmistakable sound of snow trucks doing their thing. They cleared the parking lot all right, but buried the cars even deeper. Mac jumped out of bed. "Let's go," he said. "It's time to get dressed." I dressed in my own clothes, but Mac loaned me a parka, snow boots and gloves. He went deep into his front hall closet and found two shovels. He handed one to me, and off we went into the cold. It took over an hour, but we were able to dig his car out. He put his key in the ignition and after a few scary chokes, the engine turned over. We sat together in the front seat and let the car run for awhile.

"Let's go upstairs and warm up," Mac said after a while. He locked the car and we went back into his apartment. It felt warmer and cozier than ever. Once upstairs we turned on the TV and learned that the airport was expected to open by 8 PM. My first attempts to reach the airline, met only repeated busy signals. Finally at about 5 PM, I got through. I made no attempt to get a flight for the next day, but I was able to book a late morning flight for the day after.

Once I was booked, my first call was to Tom and Dom. "Can you make dinner tomorrow evening?" I asked.

"Of course," Tom said. "I'd cancel an audience with the pope to have dinner with you guys tomorrow." We agreed to start the evening at Stoney's Bar, and decide from there where to go to dinner.

My next call was to Marsha. I told her how hard it was to reach the airline, and the earliest I could get out of Buffalo was the day after tomorrow. She was really upset and I told her how terrible I felt too. "Can you avoid business trips to Buffalo in the winter from now on?" she asked jokingly.

I needed to call my office, but it would have to wait until the morning. There was nothing left to do, but to cuddle up with Mac and do whatever nature had in mind for us. After sleeping with Mac as a couple, I was scared to think about sleeping with Marsha. Could I?

Shoveling snow had taken a toll on two old thirty somethings, and we both fell into a deep sleep. The incessant ringing of the telephone woke us both at about 8:30 AM. It was Jonathan. He said that the roads were clear enough for him to drive over, and how would we like to make him breakfast.

"Get your ass over quickly," Mac said, "and we'll hustle up some eggs."

Mac and I showered together, and dressed quickly. While Mac set the table and took out the makings of a good breakfast, I called my home office, and let them know that I would be home tomorrow, and in the office the next day.

"I'll drive you to the hotel on my way to work tomorrow and you'll have to take a cab to the airport," Mac said sadly. He came over to me and hugged me. I buried my head in his shoulder and tried hard not to cry.

When Jonathan arrived, it was obvious to us that he was in the mood for sex. We let him know that we were just too sated and he would have to wait until Thanksgiving break when Jake would be glad to take care of him. After all, Thanksgiving was only two weeks away. Poor Jonathan was disappointed, but he understood. Once the sexual tension was erased, we had a relaxing day together. We talked and talked and bonded ever closer. As the day went on, the sun began to make intermittent appearances and the temperature rose above freezing. That didn't do much for the mountain like snow mounds, but it helped clear the roadways even more.

Late in the afternoon, we informed Jonathan that we had plans for the evening, and we needed to dress.

"Sure," he said. "Wallie, have a good trip home, and don't forget to call me when you get back to Buffalo."

"Give me the address of Jake's deli," I said. One day, I'll drop in and buy something, and meet Jake. If I'm alone, I'll tell him who I am and if my wife is with me, I'll just be friendly and that will be that." Jonathan wrote an address down on a piece of paper. I slipped it in my wallet, and after a lengthy farewell filled with hugs and kisses, he was on his way.

Once again, I had to borrow a fresh shirt and a pair of trousers from Mac. Just the fact that we shared our clothing made us both horny, but we decided to wait until later. The two of us looked pretty spiffy and very handsome as we left the apartment. I couldn't help wonder why I ever thought that I would be happier pretending to be heterosexual. The fact that I was going to spend the evening with my gay lover and two gay buddies, made me feel good all over. I tried hard not to feel regret. What's done, was done, and I couldn't change it, short of leaving Marsha.

For the first time, that possibility became a viable alternative in my mind. Marsha was still young and beautiful. She would find someone who could give her a more satisfying love life than I could. I rationalized that she would actually be happier in the long run. Lucky for us, we had no children.

These thoughts elated me, and I became even happier, as if that was possible. Mac sensed how I felt. "What???" he asked.

"Nothing, I'm just happy. That's all." Mac was driving so I leaned over and kissed him on the cheek. As we drove downtown, I couldn't help but to be amazed at what a great job the city had done in clearing the snow off the roads. Back in Long Island it would have taken days, but of course, Buffalo had more practice, and probably a very big snow removal budget.

Stoney's parking lot lost several parking spaces where the snow had been piled high, but there weren't very many people venturing out yet, especially on a week night. We had no trouble parking. The bar was not at all crowded, so when we came in, I immediately spotted Tom at a corner table. He had been looking for us, and jumped up and waved.

What happened next was something I should have expected, but I wasn't prepared for. Tom grabbed me in a bear hug and kissed me full on the lips. It was less chaste a kiss than I would have thought. His tongue parted my lips and for just a moment, our tongues kissed also. I made no attempt to stop him. I knew how he felt. He was releasing all his pent up constraints and I was riding the wave with him.

When we could finally bear to let go, we made our introductions. Everyone embraced, sensing somehow that we were destined to be great friends. I was not surprised when I met Dominick. He was exactly as I had pictured him based upon Tom's description of him on the telephone. Tom was about 35 years young, but Dominick was in his early sixties. That does not mean to say that he wasn't a formidable gentleman. He stood six feet, three inches tall. Through his flannel shirt I could tell that he was lean and muscular. He had all of his hair, which was gray at the temples and black on top. His eyes were almost black. They were warm and sexually mesmerizing. I liked him immediately, and I was happy for Tom.

We ordered drinks and discussed where to eat dinner. Dominick told us that there was a wonderful Italian restaurant right around the corner that was very popular with the Italian community. They never advertised and few people outside of that community knew about it. We all agreed that it sounded great. Dom pulled out his phone and called. After a short conversation in Italian, he announced that it was a slow night and Gino was waiting for us.

We left our cars at Stoney's and walked around the corner to Gino's. I had been to Italy on my honeymoon, and had loved it. When I walked into Gino's I was transported back to Sicily. The place was a replica of many restaurants I had dined in when I was there.

Dom and Gino kissed European style, first one cheek and then the other. To my surprise, they added another kiss on the lips. Gino repeated the process with Tom, and then Dom introduced Mac and me.

"I'd like you to meet my cousin, Gino," he said to us. Then turning to Gino, he said, "These are our dear friends, Mac and Wallie." Gino kissed us both on each cheek and seated us by a working fireplace. There was no cloak room, but we hung our outer garments on a nearby clothes tree.

Gino sent over a complimentary bottle of wine, and we toasted our new found friendship. Dom made Mac promise to stay in touch with him and Tom when I went back to New York, and Mac was happy to say that he would.

The meal was superb and I am sure the other's enjoyed it, but not me. I kept thinking that my euphoria was about to come to an end. No longer would I be cuddling up to Mac as we slept. I didn't even want to think about what a farce it is that I was sleeping with Marsha, but I couldn't keep my brain clear of those thoughts. As the meal progressed, I became more and more morose. Mac had to have noticed because he grabbed my hand and before we even had dessert, he said, "You know it's been absolutely amazing meeting you guys, but this is our last night together for awhile, so please excuse us if we take off right after dessert."

Tom must have noticed my mood change also, and he said, "Not at all, Mac. We understand." Then he winked at me and said, "I just know the Buffalo office will be needing you more and more, Wallie. I'll see to it."

Mac and I had spumoni for dessert, gave Tom money for our bill, and then we said our good byes. Lots of hugs and kisses, even from Gino, who begged us to return again soon. We promised that we would.

Driving home, we were both very silent. Mac broke that silence by saying, "Let's make it a memorable night, sweetheart."

I smiled and said, "Yes, let's."

Minutes after we got home we were naked, and stepping into the shower. I grabbed the soap first and began to lather Mac all over. I just kept soaking his cock over and over, and then I soaped his crack. As I did so, one finger and then two, found themselves sliding up Mac's ass hole. He sighed loudly and leaned into me. My middle finger found his prostate and his sigh became a moan.

"If you don't stop, I'll cum," he said emphatically. I kept my finger in his hole and got down on my knees. I took his cock into my mouth and continued to play with his prostate. Mac leaned his back against the shower wall for support. Apparently his knees were buckling. He came, screaming loudly. The tile wall of the shower reverberated with his scream and made it sound even louder. His cum filled me up and it tasted warm and comforting. I stood up and Mac leaned against me.

He took the soap from the tray and soaped his ass until it was a willing receptacle. At long last he turned his back to me and urged me to enter him. I soaped my cock a little more, placed the head at his crack, and pushed in easily. "Don't move," Mac begged me. "Let me just enjoy the feel of you for a bit." Our intentions were good. I held still for a long time, but little by little we started to gyrate. I moved my cock in and out, and once again, I manipulated Mac's prostate with my throbbing cock.

"I don't believe it," he moaned. "I'm cumming again." Then he roared his blood curdling scream as he spurted against the shower wall. As he came, his ass hole constricted, and that put me past the point of no return. A fraction of a second later, I came up his ass. I was bucking and screaming as loud as Mac. We didn't move until my cock fell out all by itself.

We washed down the shower walls and cleaned ourselves of love's evidence. We dried ourselves off and went to bed. We slept wrapped together. One moment we played with our cocks and balls. The next moment we played with our nipples. For hours we kissed, hugged and titillated each other, until eventually we fell asleep. During the entire evening of love making, I didn't think of Marsha once.

Mac and I had agreed that when he dropped me off at the hotel, I would hustle right out of the car. There would be no long kisses and sobby farewells. "This is it," I said as he pulled over in front of the hotel. I jumped out of the car and practically ran up to my room.

As I was packing my bag, I thought of calling Tom to see if there was anything last minute at the office which would require my attention. He sounded so glad to hear my voice.

"Just a sec," he said. "I want to close my door." After a moment, he was back on the line. "What did you think of Dominick?" he asked me.

"He's first rate. You're both lucky, and I gotta tell you, he's very sexy. You better watch him like a hawk."

"Your Mac is a hunk," he added. "I immediately got the hots for him. We'll have to do a four way some day." I didn't know if he was kidding or not, and I had no intention of asking. Instead, I told him how glad I was that we had discovered the truth about each other. We chatted briefly and as we said goodbye, I was prompted to conclude with, "I love you, Tommy."

"Wait," he yelled. "Don't hang up! What time are you leaving for the airport?"

"In about half an hour," I answered.

"Don't take a cab. I'll shoot right over and drive you there. I've got time, and Wallie, I really want to do that. It will give me a chance to talk to you. You may not want it, but Dom and I have some practical advice for you."

"Sure," I said. "I'll go down to the lobby and I'll keep an eye out for you."

As Tom drove up about twenty minutes later, he honked his horn and I ran to his car. "Throw your stuff on the back seat," he ordered, "and hop in. Once inside, I put on my seat belt and settled in for the ride to the airport.

Tom wasted no time. "Dom and I have been talking," he began. "It's a crime to live your life like this. Both Dom and I are in the closet only at work, and even that's a fucking burden. We can't imagine you living every aspect of your life totally closeted. You've got to be free to go places with Mac, to live with him, to double date with friends, both straight and gay, and spend happy social evenings with members of the gay community. We could both see how agonized you were last night, and we cried for you."

"It's exactly as you describe it," I said. "But what can I do about it?"

"You know what you have to do, but it will take courage. Be grateful you have no children. Marsha will be better off also. She deserves to be fucked by someone who is enjoying it, and is not pretending. Find the courage, dear friend, and leave your marriage. You and Mac will find happiness and so will Marsha, in time."

"I know you're right, Tom, but I'm scared shitless. If I do leave her, do I tell her the real reason or make up another lie?"

"The truth is always the safest and best route to take. I know what's best, theoretically, but Wallie baby, I'm glad I'm not you. At least you have three shoulders to cry on and to support you," Tom said.

"Actually, I have two more shoulders. Jonathan Mallory and I have become good friends. Mac has been mentoring him in how to function as a gay man (that was vague enough) and he and his partner are another source of support."

"That's great," Tom said. We were just turning into the airport, and Tom said, "Please keep me informed of everything, no matter what you decide to do." He got out of the car with me and helped me get my stuff from the rear seat. He hugged me, got back in the car and drove off. I stood there staring after his disappearing car until I heard the curbside checker ask me if he could take my bag.

Marsha met me at LaGuardia and she kept hugging and kissing me and telling me how much she missed me. She wasn't making it easy for me to consider leaving her. When we got home, she insisted that I take a nap before dinner. I figured out quickly what that was all about. She wanted me well rested for sex that night.

God! I thought. Do I have anything left in me? I really was exhausted and I took her up on her suggestion that I take a nap. I lay down in bed, knowing full well that I would never fall asleep. Then the thought came to me.

What if I can't perform tonight? What if I could never perform again? What if Marsha caught me in bed with a man? Would she want to leave me? The thought was far-fetched but comforting, and I actually fell asleep.

Chapter Six

During the next two months, I travelled to Cleveland and St. Louis, but Buffalo was not on the agenda. I kept in constant touch with Mac. We cried a lot, whacked off a lot together on the phone, and we were generally two miserable individuals. It was comforting to know, but I was extremely jealous, that he and Jonathan were making it together as often as possible. In between business trips, I managed to have sex with Marsha about once a week. I could sense that she was beginning to be dissatisfied and I was secretly happy about that.

One Saturday, she went to a day spa with our next door neighbor. The neighbor's husband was stuck with the kids, but I was free to come and go. I decided that it would be a good day to visit Jake McLean. I drove to Oceanside and found the deli. The store was really crowded. There were at least five people behind the counter, and at least six tiers of customers. How was I ever going to speak to Jake? I pushed my way to the front, and spotted him behind the counter. He was even prettier than I remembered him at the airport. I had sex with his partner, and I wouldn't mind a little bit of action with him.

I did not take a number, preferring to wait until the crowd let up. The store hours were posted, and on Saturday they closed at 3 PM. I figured the crowds would let up by noon, and then I could get hold of the beautiful guy behind the counter. I didn't have to wait that long. At about 10 AM, Jake did not serve the next customer. Instead he went through a door to the back of the store. I ran to the door and before Jake could close it, I grabbed the handle.

"What the hell!" he said.

"I'm sorry, Jake, but I need to talk to you," I said. "I'm a good friend of Jonathan's. My name is Jonathan Walters, Wallie."

"Holy mother of God," Jake almost screamed. "Jonathan has told me all about you. I feel like I've known you for years." He held the door open and beckoned me to come into the back room. The room was full of meats, cheeses and fresh breads. The aroma of the room almost gave me an orgasm. In a far corner of the room, a small office was partitioned off. There was a bathroom in the office. Jake took me to the office and closed the door.

"Excuse me," he said. "I have to pee badly." He opened the bathroom door and began to pee without closing the door. His cock was a replica of Jonathan's and I began to get hard. It was uncut and well sized. When he was done, he shook it off, replaced it and washed his hands. Then he came up to me and to my happy surprise he hugged me and kissed me on the lips.

"That was nice," I said, "but what for?"

"That's for you and Mac teaching Jonathan all those wonderful new tricks. When he came home for Thanksgiving, I couldn't believe what he did for us. By Christmas vacation, our sex life became a fantasy world come true, and I owe it to you and Mac." He gave me another kiss.

"Well, it was mostly Mac who had the pleasure of teaching, but I had the pleasure of allowing him to practice on me." We both laughed at that. "You know, Jonathan is like a son to me, so that makes you my son in law. Maybe I should start calling him, junior." We both laughed again.

"Listen," Jake said, "I can break away about noon. The crowds let up then. I have a couple of high school kids working for me part time. I'll ask them to stay a little extra. Will you be able to spend a couple of hours with me this afternoon and we'll get to know each other?"

"I'd love that," I said. "While I'm waiting, I think I'll buy some deli to take home." The smells out there have me salivating." We went out front and Jake waited on me, much to the displeasure of some of the customers on line. He refused to take money from me and when I protested, he said. "I can't take money from my father in law." Those customers who heard that were assuaged a little bit from their anger at my having cut into line. I purchased a pound of ham, a pound of Genoa salami, a pound of kosher salami, a half pound of Swiss cheese and a dozen New York hard rolls. I wanted to buy some chopped liver, but I was afraid it wouldn't hold up until I got home. I put everything on the back seat of my car. It seemed cold enough outside, if I wanted to buy the chopped liver, but I decided in the end not to do it. That would give me a reason to return another time.

A little before noon, Jake removed his apron and came out from behind the counter. "My dad's closing up today so we can get going. I just got my own apartment only a block away, so that when Jonathan comes home, we now have our own private hang out. Come, we can walk there."

Do your parents know about you two?" I stupidly asked, as we approached his building.

"They've known since we first met, and both sets of parents are cool with it. In fact our parents have become best friends and consider themselves to be in laws."

"That's great," I said. Once again, I cursed my own timidity which had put me into my present situation.

Jake's apartment was small, but very cozy. It had one fair sized bedroom, a small living room and a pretty big eat in kitchen. "I'll make lunch," he said. "How about a deli sandwich?"

"That's about what I would have expected," I laughed. Jake motioned for me to sit at the kitchen table. He set out plates, flatware and napkins.

"Soda or beer?" he asked.

"Beer sounds good with deli," I answered.

Jake made us salami on rye sandwiches. He put the beer and deli mustard on the table and we sat down to eat together. The sandwich was delicious, but I kept thinking that Jake would taste even more delicious. Being the older of the two of us, I figured I should be the aggressive one.

"I wouldn't be telling tales out of school, if I told you that Mac and Jonathan are having sex regularly. They have been open about it, and I'm all right with it. How about you?"

"Same here. Mac has done nothing but bring my own sex life to new heights. But in the meantime, I have to satisfy myself with phone sex. We had three way phone sex last week."

"That's fantastic," I said. "That hasn't happened to me yet, but I intend to remedy that situation."

Unexpectedly, Jake put his hand on mine. " I think that it would be very appropriate if we did what our guys are doing. Don't you think?" he asked.

'You don't have to ask me twice," I said. We both jumped up, and abandoning our half eaten sandwiches and our partially consumed beers, we grabbed each other in a bone crushing bear hug. Our lips met, and our tongues found each other. We explored our mouths as if we didn't know what a mouth tasted like.

Moments later we were lying naked in Jake's bed. "Let me show you what Jonathan taught me," he whispered in my ear.

"Show me. I can't wait." He began to give me a trip around the world, front and back, which lasted almost an hour. My eyes were closed, and it was easy to picture Mac doing the honors. The technique was exactly the same and for good reason. When there was not a spot on my body, he hadn't licked with his tongue, he took me into his mouth.

"Oh Mac," I whispered. "That's wonderful." In spite of my blunder of calling him, Mac, Jake didn't miss a beat.

"I'm getting close," I said to him, and he stopped sucking my cock. He got a condom and lube from his night table drawer, and handed them to me. "I like it doggie style," he said. "If you don't mind."

He turned over and got himself on all fours. He grabbed two pillows and supported his head with them. I put on the condom and greased my cock. Then I put lube on my finger and lubed his ass hole. I straddled this hunk, growing crazier by the minute. I tried to go in slowly, but I was so worked up that I started to just ramrod right in. Jake flinched for just a second, but I fell into his pit rather easily. I held still waiting for him to get used to me.

"Fuck me as hard as you can," he said to my surprise, so I started in and out, never once letting my cock head fall out of his ass. No matter how hard I thrust, Jake yelled, "Harder, harder." That was good for me too, and I came rather quickly, filling up the condom.

After awhile we flushed the soaking condom down the toilet and wiped Jake's ass clean. We lay side by side holding hands and saying nothing. Finally Jake said, "Would you mind if I came in your mouth, instead of your ass, this time. I want you to taste me."

"I wouldn't mind at all," I said. "It would be a pleasure." It wasn't hard for me to fantasize that I was with Mac. Their cocks were both uncut, and about the same size and girth. While I was pleasuring Jake, and me for that matter, I realized that he had used the phrase *this time*. That meant that Jake expected us to do this again and that was OK with me also.

When he came, Jake gave me so much cum, that I could not swallow all of it. I swallowed what I could. The rest ran down his cock and his pubic area. I scooped some up on my finger and offered it to him. He took it greedily.

We lay side by side trying to recover and basking in the afterglow of good, no, superior sex. We begin to kiss. Our tongues explored each other's mouths and our teeth nipped and teased our necks. "We need to tell Jonathan and Mac about this or it won't be all right," Jake said.

Without answering him, I reached for my cell phone on Jake's night table and phoned Mac. It went to his answering machine, so he was either in the middle of an investigation or he was fucking Jonathan. Because I had a tinge of guilt, I prayed it was Jonathan. I left a two word message, "Call me."

I handed the phone to Jake who proceeded to call Jonathan. Jonathan answered on the first ring. He was in his dorm studying. "Hi love," Jake said. "Wallie just fucked me and I came in his mouth." Without giving Jonathan a chance to respond, he continued. "I love him. He insists that he is our daddy and we are his sons. I love the thought."

"I know how you feel," Jonathan said. "I love him too. Let me talk to him."

Jake handed me the phone. "Hi, Junior," I quipped. "Watchya doing?"

"Studying, pops. I don't have to ask what you're doing. Are you in Jake's little love nest?"

"Yup, and I'm trying to reach Mac. He's not answering his cell phone."

"I can't help you there. I haven't spoken to him today at all, and he was supposed to call me about dinner tonight," Jonathan said.

"OK. I love you," I said, as I handed the phone back to Jake.

"I love you too," Jake told his lover. "I'm trying to get my dad to cover for me over a weekend soon, so I can get up to visit you. Spring break is just too far away."

"Make it soon, my darling. Mac said we could stay in his apartment."

"I'm working on it. Until then, I love you with all my heart and soul." He started to cry and he hung up the phone. I pulled him to me and held him tightly, until he stopped crying.

The clock on his night table said that it was 5:30. "I gotta go," I said regretfully. I got out of bed and started to dress. When I had my trousers on, I took my card out of my wallet. "Call me anytime on my cell phone," I implored, and let's get together again soon. You're a life saver."

"You're a life saver for me too," Jake said. "Why don't you take up squash?"

"What?" I wondered what Jake was driving at, with such a strange question.

"Tell your wife, that some of the guys at work are taking up the game and you'll be playing with them a couple of evenings a week and Saturday afternoons. She won't like it, but it will give us opportunities to get together. You name the two evenings a week, and I'll make myself available to you."

"She's already beginning to show me that she's unhappy at our infrequent sex, and the poor quality of the sex when we do have it. This will irk her even more. I've got to work up my courage and tell her some day soon that I'm gay, and our only solution is to divorce. I just don't have the balls yet."

"Don't wait too long. She's getting older every day. Let her go free while she's still young and attractive. When you are ready, maybe we can arrange to have her catch us together. She'll kick you out for sure. After she does, you're welcome to stay here until you figure out what you and Mac want to do."

"That's funny," I said. "I had thought the same thing recently, about getting caught, I mean. Then I wouldn't have to be brave and tell her anything. Like they say, 'a picture is worth a thousand words.'"

"You should be braver about your life and your future," Jake said sternly. "You're one of the good guys and you deserve to be happy the rest of your life. Don't keep waiting to get your courage up. Create courage."

I started to cry and Jake wrapped his arms around me in an attempt to console me in what I considered to be an inconsolable situation. He was holding me tightly when my cell phone rang. I looked at it and smiled at him. "It's Mac," I said.

"This one's unbelievable," he said. "Some jerk shot his wife right down town on McKinley Circle in full view of hundreds of people. Then he just stood there and waited for the police. He not only killed his wife, he killed my whole afternoon. I was supposed to spend it with Jonathan, but now I'm on my way to meet him for dinner."

"Good," I said, "because Jake and I finally met, and we had each other for lunch and dessert. Suffice it to say, we were both so horny, we couldn't resist each other. Jake has already told Jonathan. I'm glad we spoke before you met him for dinner."

"Wow!" Mac said. "That's big news indeed. I've got something along those lines to ask you. Tom and Dominick have been hinting that we should have a three way, and when you get here, a four way. How does that grab you?"

"Tom's like a brother to me," I said. "I'll have to think about it. In the meantime, if you would like to have fun, I'm all for it. Just keep on loving me."

"I'll never stop," Mac assured me. "As for sleeping with your brother, we are already sleeping with our sons."

"How true, and I am really enjoying it." I hesitated for a moment and then said, "Mac, honey, I am giving serious thought to telling Marsha that I am gay and that I need to divorce her. I'm really getting convinced that no matter what she says, she'll be better off."

"Honey, I'm not pushing it, but it would be so wonderful. I love you so much and living on stolen moments isn't fair to either of us," Mac said with authority.

All the way home, I rehearsed possible scenarios of how to tell Marsha about my sexual preference, but each scenario had flaws and continued to scare me to death. I was convinced that having her find me naked in bed with Jake was a bad idea; still it was the least scary.

I was pleased to see that I got home before Marsha did. I put the meat and cheese in the fridge and the rolls in the breadbox. I figured we could have deli for dinner and I would freeze the left over meat and rolls. I called her on her cell phone and she told me that she would be home in about fifteen minutes.

I went about setting the table, and I figured to remove the food from the fridge when we sat down to dinner. While waiting for Marsha, I turned on the TV and watched the evening news. For all Marsha could tell I had been sitting home like this all afternoon.

She literally floated into the house, all bubbly and refreshed from her day at the spa. I stood up to kiss her and as she approached me her whole demeanor changed. Instead of a kiss, I was greeted with a big slap on the face. There were tears in her eyes.

"Bastard," she yelled as she ran upstairs to our bedroom. I heard the door slam shut.

What in the world did she see on me that gave me away. Obviously my afternoon indiscretion was clear to her. I walked over to the big mirror in the living room and stared in disbelief. On my neck was the biggest hickey I had ever gotten or seen, and I was totally unaware of it. It was the size of a half dollar and as purple as a plum. I began to shake like a leaf, but I also realized that I would never have a better opportunity to come out with the truth.

I climbed the stairs slowly and knocked softly on our bedroom door. I got no response so I opened the door. Marsha was lying face up on the bed.

She was not crying and she appeared perfectly calm. She was staring at the ceiling, barely moving or blinking her eyes.

"We need to talk," I said.

"Who is she, and when did you stop loving me?"

"I never stopped loving you," I protested. "I'll love you until the day I die, but there is something I must tell you." That statement must have piqued her interest. She didn't move her body, but she turned to look at me. Her eyes fixed on mine. I wanted to tell her the truth, but still I hesitated.

"Well tell me whatever lame excuse you want to," she sneered.

"No excuses," I said. "Here's the truth. Maybe it would be more accurate to say, here's the problem between us, and no amount of my loving you can change that. Marsha honey, I'm gay."

At first there was no reaction from her, but then she burst out laughing. "If you're gay," she giggled, "I'm The Virgin Mary. You can do better than that."

I took my wallet out of my pocket and groped for the secret compartment. I pulled out a picture of Mac that I had taken with his digital camera when we were snowbound in his apartment. He was totally naked, but his cock was discreetly hidden by a book. I showed it to Marsha.

"This is Mac," I said. "He's my lover."

Marsha stared at the picture. She seemed frozen in time. She stared for what seemed to me to be forever. Then she gave out a blood curdling scream.

"Get out," she yelled. "I hate you. I never want to see you again. The next time you hear from me, it will be through a lawyer. She rolled over the bed and grabbed the phone on the table. For a second I thought she was going to throw it at me, but she started to punch in a number.

I have no idea why I asked her, but I asked who she was calling. Maybe I was afraid she was calling a hit man.

"If you must know, I'm calling my cousin Louise. I want to get the number of the lawyer she used in her divorce. He took her husband for everything."

"That won't be necessary," I said. "You can have whatever you want. You can have everything. I won't fight you. I'll give you everything I own. It's a cheap price to pay for my identity."

"Come here," Marsha said. I approached her and she spit in my face. Frankly, I could not blame her.

I packed three suitcases and my toiletries, and put them in the trunk of my car. I drove a few blocks and then I pulled the car over. I got out Jake's number and called him. Thank God he was home.

"Can you put me up for a day or two?" I asked. "Marsha kicked me out."

"Of course, I can, but how did this happen. I didn't think you quite had the courage to tell her yet."

"Well, it seems you gave me one hell of a hickey. At first she thought it was a woman, but I finally told her the truth."

"Gee, I'm sorry." Jake said. "It must have come out after you left me or I certainly would have warned you." He repeated several times, "I'm so sorry. I'm so sorry."

"Don't be sorry," I implored him. "It was as good as her catching us in bed together. From now on, you can give me as many hickey's as you want to."

"Stop talking, and get your ass over here. I could use a little more of your magical tongue."

"We'll call the guys and my friend Tom when I get there. Is your store open on Sundays?"

"Yes," he answered. "But Sunday is my day off."

"I'm off too," I said. "I just have a feeling that you'll know exactly how to soothe my troubled soul."

Chapter Seven

As soon as I got to Jake's apartment, and brought in my meager belongings, I called Mac on my cell phone, and Jake called Jonathan on his land phone. While I was telling Mac everything that had transpired, thanks to an accidental hickey, he was so silent, that several times I had to ask if he was still there.

When I was all finished, there was still a frightening silence. Finally he said or rather, he croaked, "I just can't talk right now. I'm too emotional. All my prayers are coming true. I'll call you back in the morning. In the meantime I'm going to take some time off next weekend and come down to New York. Tell Jake, I'll try to bring Jonathan with me. I'm sorry but I gotta hang up right now before I lose it." Click.

I didn't want him to hang up. I wanted to talk all night, but I resigned my self to waiting until the next day to talk to Mac. When I hung up, Jake was still talking to Jonathan. He was laughing and smiling and I could hear Jonathan bubbling at the other end.

"Please let me talk to Jonathan for a minute," I pleaded with Jake.

"Sure," he said as he handed me the phone.

"Jonathan," I began, "Mac is so emotional I'm afraid he's not thinking clearly. Can you look in on him tonight, please."

"That won't be necessary," he said. "We're at Stoney's right now, and then we're meeting Tom and Dominick at Gino's for dinner. I assure you, Mac is fine. He's just sitting here and crying in his beer."

"Please hold him and kiss him for me, and please fill Tom in on everything. I was just about to call him, but I'm pretty done out myself, and would appreciate it if you handled it for me." I gave the phone back to Jake and he and Jonathan said a quick farewell.

Suddenly my emotions erupted into a torrent of tears. Jake held me in his arms, rocking me back and forth.

"I have a great idea," he said. "Let's have a nice dinner out like our guys are doing. My treat! What's your favorite cuisine?" he asked.

"Chinese," I said. He handed me my coat and I followed him out the door.

When we got back to his apartment, Jake insisted that I soak in a nice hot tub. He was kind enough to run the bath water, and I was happy to step in. The hot water did indeed feel wonderful. While I was just sitting there, feeling good, Jake got undressed. He got on his knees at the edge of the tub. He had a wash cloth in his hands, which he wet, and he began to soap it up. Then he began to wash me like I was a babe in a bassinet. God, wherever he touched me it felt wonderful, but eventually he reached my balls and I realized that I was going to be able to have sex with Jake after all. I had been afraid that in light of the evening's events, I wouldn't be able to get aroused. He got hold of my cock and peeled back my foreskin. Gently, he washed my head clean and soaped it up good. By now I was as hard as ever I got.

"You're going to smell like a whore," he said.

"As long as it pleases you," I replied.

Jake stood up and pulled a very large bath towel out of the linen closet. He held it up, and I stepped out of the tub and into the towel. He wrapped the towel around me and began to pat me dry. He seemed determined to do all the work and cater to me, and I was content to allow it.

When I was dry, Jake put me in his bed, shut the light, and climbed in next to me. He wrapped himself around me, and whispered, "I want you to rest now and try to get some sleep. We have plenty of time to make love." We grew silent and both of us dozed off.

I was so emotionally drained that I slept all night. Jake woke up about 6 AM, but he stayed in bed so as not to disturb me. He nestled up against me and wrapped his arms around my torso. Even in my sleep, I felt warm and protected.

About 8 AM, I was awakened by the ringing of Jake's doorbell. Jake jumped out of bed. "Who the hell can that be at this hour?" he mumbled as he grabbed his robe and ran to the door. I just lay there in bed, groggy, still unable to move. I heard Jake scream and I sat up quickly in bed. Two figures were running into the room and looked ready to pounce on me. It was Mac and Jonathan.

They smothered me with hugs and kisses. I was naked and should have gotten hard as a rock, but I had to pee so badly that I could only get a semi erect piss hardon.

"We had dinner last night with Tom and Dominick," Mac explained. "They were thrilled when they heard the news, and it was they who pointed out that if we got in a car immediately, we could drive the approximate 450 miles in seven to eight hours, stopping only for gas and to pee. We excused ourselves, went to my apartment, packed an overnight bag for the two of us, made some sandwiches and headed for the Thruway. Tada! Here we are. I'll call in sick tomorrow and Jonathan will cut a couple of classes. We'll leave about 5 PM and we'll get back to Buffalo around midnight or a little later."

Mac took my head in his hands and totally ignored my morning breath by kissing me hard on the lips. I looked at him helplessly.

"I would love to show you right this minute, in front of these two fine sons of ours, just how much I love you, but I have to pee so badly, you'd better let go of me."

While this was going on Jake and Jonathan were locked in a never ending embrace and Jonathan's clothes were falling slowly to the floor.

"Not now," I yelled as I emerged from the bathroom. "First we are going out for brunch. Sunday brunch in New York is a not to be missed experience."

"Good idea," Jonathan agreed. "I'm starved. We finished off the sandwiches hours ago. I slept in the car when Mac drove, but I could use a little nap time too."

We all dressed and headed for a nearby diner. While we were waiting for our orders, Jonathan walked outside and made a phone call. When he returned, he informed us that he and Jake were going to sleep at his parents' home this evening and Mac and I could have the apartment to ourselves.

"We'll join you tomorrow morning," Jake said with a wink and a grin.

We ate so much at the diner that we agreed that there would be no lunch, but we would consider going out for dinner. When we got back to the apartment, we put Mac and Jonathan to sleep in Jake's bed. The four of us agreed on a three hour maximum. Jake and I closed the bedroom door and went into the living room.

We sat close to each other on the sofa. "How do you feel now that it's all sinking in?" Jake asked me.

"Happy, at peace, euphoric, and scared shitless," I answered truthfully. "I feel like shouting out the window, *I'm gay in every sense of the word, and I have the most beautiful boy friend a guy could have. If you don't like it then fuck you!*"

Jake laughed and kissed me on the lips. While our lovers were napping, I took the opportunity to call Tom and Dominick. They had just walked into the house from church when I reached them.

"If there's anything we can do to help you get through this, you know we are here for you," Tom said. "We love you, and right now we are so happy for you, but at the same time we are very concerned."

"Thanks bro," I said. "I know you mean it and I appreciate it."

"Is Jake available?" Tom asked. "I'd like to introduce myself and say hello."

"Yes, he's right here." I handed the phone to Jake.

"Hi Jake," Tom said. "This is Uncle Tommy."

"And Uncle Dominick," Dom piped in from the background.

Tom continued. "We have grown to know and to love Jonathan and through him, we already love you. I can't wait to meet you. In the meantime see to it that Mac and Jonathan have a bang up weekend. Until we meet, ciao."

We gave the guys three hours, but they were up in two. Jonathan came out of the bedroom and told me to go in.

"Jake and I will use the couch. You old guys can use the bed," Jonathan said. I tapped him on his tush as I sprinted toward the bedroom. I didn't bother to shut the door. I undressed and jumped into bed with Mac."

He wrapped himself around me. His hard cock tried to ram my thigh and I almost swooned from the joy I felt. I caressed his back and his ass cheeks, but I was too full of emotion to speak.

"Are you going to be OK?" Mac asked me.

"With you at my side, nothing can harm me. My big strong cop will protect me."

"Do you have a lawyer?" he asked.

"It just so happens that my sister's husband is a divorce attorney, but I don't want to fight Marsha. She can have whatever I can give her except my company car."

(Months later, in the divorce settlement, Marsha did get almost everything. She lost out on one point only. The judge denied her claim for alimony. My lawyer had convinced the judge that since she had an MS in Clinical Psychology and no children, she was perfectly capable of making a living. And if that were not enough, I had given her everything I had, far more than was legally required.)

"Stop worrying about me," I told Mac, "and fuck me until I scream for mercy." I reached into the drawer where I knew Jake had lubricant and handed it to Mac. He leered at me like the villain in an old silent movie and twirled an imaginary handle bar mustache. Then the love making began.

About two hours later, Jonathan appeared at the door. Jake is waiting to get better acquainted with you, Mac, so head for the couch and let me at that hunk next to you.

I was really done out for at least several hours, but when you are as young as Jonathan, recovery is fast. He was all set to go again, so I went down on him to get his juices flowing and then I let him fuck me. After that, I think that he was done for awhile also. We lay in bed exhausted. I held his hand and we whispered to each other how much we loved each other. I almost dozed off when Mac and Jake bounded in. There was hardly room in the bed, but our bodies twisted and turned and somehow all four of us occupied the bed. It was lovely to be lying here all tied up with the ones I loved most in the world. It didn't even bother me to know that somewhere close by, Marsha was alone and weeping.

The four of us spent a good part of the day in the one bed, hugging, caressing, kissing, rimming, sucking, and the youngsters even fucked Mac and me again. Even though I love Jake and Jonathan, I looked forward to being alone with Mac. There was so much to talk about and to plan.

Early in the evening, we showered two at a time. We all dressed casually. Mac and Jonathan had very few wardrobe changes with them. Jake and Jonathan took us to a well known sea food restaurant in Oceanside. It was quite crowded and we had to wait about forty-five minutes to be seated. We waited at the bar, and much to their consternation, the boys were carded. That gave Mac and me a good laugh.

The restaurant bought live lobsters daily from the local fishermen. We each picked out a likely looking lobster from the tank and the sea monsters were prepared to our orders. It was well worth the wait. We all donned bibs and went to work. We attacked every part of the lobster and I would defy anyone to have found an ort of meat left when we were finished. As wonderful as the meal was, all I could think of was that Mac was mine, all mine, really mine. I kept looking at him and smiling, thinking that he was the handsomest dude in the room; the best looking cop in the USA. I had shed my foolish desire to be a cog in the mainstream. I was gay and I was fulfilled. I didn't care who knew it or how they reacted to it. I was I!!! It was all true.

At the end of the meal none of us could move. Mac and I shared the check, ignoring the objections of our two boys. Even though I figured that Jake might make a better living than either Mac or I, I felt that it was our duty as parents to pick up the check.

When we finally left the restaurant, Jake drove us to his apartment and dropped us off. The boys went on to Jonathan's parents.

"We'll be here early tomorrow," Jake said before they left. "I've got plenty of food in the house and we'll have breakfast in. I called my father and told him that Jonathan surprised me with a short visit, and he's going to cover for me in the store tomorrow. The rest of you can call in sick or whatever you have to do. Ta, ta." He threw a kiss at both of us.

We entered the apartment with Jake's key and locked the door behind us. Mac grabbed me and hugged me and I felt like I had died and gone to heaven. I grabbed his hand and headed for the bedroom. "Wait," he said, "I have something important to talk to you about."

"God," I said. "You're not dumping me, are you? Not now. Not now that I'm free." I sincerely meant what I said. My insecurity knew no bounds.

"Sure I'm dumping you, you idiot. That's why I travelled all night to be with you." He grabbed me and began kissing me again. I swear his tongue went down my throat. "This has to do with our future as a couple."

"That's different," I said relieved. "Talk."

"Last week I searched the internet for openings in this area for detectives. I found two opening in Valley Stream, right next door from here. I faxed a résumé and they called me two hours later. They interviewed me on the phone and said that the job was mine if I wanted it, but they would need to interview me face to face to seal the deal. It pays a lot more than I am making now. I was supposed to come down next Friday. I made it for Friday hoping you could get away from Marsha for a few hours over the weekend. Now, I'll call them tomorrow and see if they will interview me tomorrow. If not, I'll be back next weekend."

I was speechless.

"Aren't you going to say anything?" Mac sounded concerned.

"Yeah. Even if you interview tomorrow and get the job, come down next weekend anyway, and we'll look for an apartment in Valley Stream. It's an easy commute to Manhattan from there. It's much shorter than the trip I had from Massapequa."

"I love you Jonathan Walters, and I'm giddy at the fact that our lives are coming together, and taking the same course for the future."

"You talk too much," I said. "Show me!"

"Come," he said. "This will be the first time as a married couple. I promise to give you a wedding night you'll never forget." He did and I'll never forget it.

At his insistence, Mac did all the work. He brought me off a record three times that night, by mouth and by ass. At the end I could barely speak.

"Damn, I'm good," he said. "After you have rested do you think you could do as much for me?"

"I hope so. Anyway, I always accept a meaningful challenge."

The boys arrived about 9:00 AM just as Mac was getting off the phone. He had called the Valley Stream precinct's human resources department, and they had set him up for an 11 AM interview. Mac figured that it would include lunch so that they could get to know him in a social setting as well as a professional one. We told the boys what was going on with Mac's interview. They were very excited, not only for Mac and me, but for themselves as well.

"I'll drive you over there," Jake said, "but for now Chef Jacob McLean is going to work his magic. I want everyone out of my way while I work. Jonathan you can set the table, and set up the coffee while I cook."

Jake prepared French toast sprinkled with cinnamon and shaved almonds. He put three kinds of syrups on the table; maple, raspberry and strawberry. Shades of IHOP! Jonathan poured four glasses of orange juice, and started the coffee maker. The aroma in the kitchen was intoxicating, as if I needed further intoxication. At that moment in time, I was happier than I had ever been in my life. Sex was not even a factor in the equation. All that was happening was that a close knit family was enjoying breakfast together.

We lingered over breakfast and talked a lot about our plans for the future. That's when Jonathan dropped the next bombshell. "I'm transferring to LIU next semester," he said. "I didn't want to say anything until I was sure they would accept me. I can live right here with you, Jake, and commute to school."

Jake jumped up and grabbed Jonathan, pulling him so close they looked like they would meld together. He was speechless, but there were tears in his eyes.

"I didn't think it would be so hard to be separated," Jonathan said.

"Neither did I," Jake echoed the sentiment.

When it was time for Jake to drive Mac to his interview, Jonathan and I set about cleaning up the breakfast mess. The last plate was put away, and the place was looking ship shape when Jake returned. "Mac will call when it's over and we can all go get him. In the meantime," he said, "we have two or three hours before he'll call. How about we play a little?" Without waiting for an answer, he began to strip, and then Jonathan followed suit. I was slower to respond so they started to undress me right there in the living room until I was naked. We didn't bother to go to the bedroom. They both fell to their knees and began to suck my cock and my balls at the same time. This morning when I woke up I thought I would be unable to get an erection for at least a week, but here I was, hard as a rock again, and definitely feeling an orgasm coming on.

"You guys are killing me," I cried. "I'm loving it."

They pulled me to the floor and we formed a daisy chain. None of us stopped sucking until each of us came. Afterward, we lay on the floor hugging, kissing and fondling. None of us discriminated as to who was hugging, kissing or fondling whom. Our love extended to all present and to the one at the police station.

The phone rang at about 2:30 PM. "I start working here three weeks from today," Mac announced. "Now come pick me up. We don't have much time left." We cheered for him, and reluctantly we dressed and went to get him.

When he got into the back seat of Jake's car, he kissed me hard. "Everything is falling into place," he told me. "I've got a lot of work to do when I get home. I'll put everything in storage until we find a place. I hope you like my furniture, honey, since you don't have a stitch of your own."

"I like everything about you," I let him know "and that includes your furniture."

"Listen guys," Mac continued, "I got a weather report for the length of the Thruway at the police station. It's snowing heavily between Syracuse and Rochester and it's headed toward Buffalo. I think Jonathan and I should leave as soon as we get back to Jake's place."

Everyone agreed. "I'll make you sandwiches and give you a cooler with cokes. That way, you'll only have to stop for gas and to pee."

Back at the apartment, Mac and Jonathan packed their overnight bag. We put the bag, cooler and the sandwiches in the back seat. We said our teary goodbyes, and Mac promised to come to New York on Friday since he already had his plane tickets, which he had purchased for his interview.

It was about 3:45 PM when they left, and if the roads were good, they would get home before midnight. Jonathan drove first because he knew his way around the city and would take them to the Thruway. After that, they would alternate driving.

Jake and I stood in the street and waved goodbye as they drove off. Suddenly I was overcome with a feeling of pure dread and foreboding. It was so bad I needed to barf and ran back inside to do so. Fortunately the desire to vomit passed, but the terrible feeling of dread did not.

That night, neither Jake nor I were in the mood for sex, but we were lying in bed holding hands and watching the news, when the telephone rang, and I feared that something terrible had happened.

Chapter Eight

Everything was too good to be true!! Something terrible had happened to spoil things. It is a testament to how much I was unable to accept my good fortune that my fear and my paranoia were in over drive. My heart stopped beating as Jake picked up the phone. I stared at his face for any sign of bad news. I was ready to kill myself if anything had happened to Mac or Jonathan. In my mind's eye, I could see Mac's car crashing into a telephone pole or into an oncoming car in a blinding snow storm. I was shaking and I couldn't breathe.

It seemed like an hour passed before Jake said, "Hello." I could hear a voice on the other end of the line, but I couldn't tell who it was or what was being said. I tried to read Jake's face, but it was a blank page. I tried to tell myself that he wasn't as paranoid or as fearful as I was, and that's why I couldn't read his face.

"That was a smart thing to do. Here's Wallie," Jake said as he handed me the phone. He didn't say who it was, and I expected a voice to say, "This is State Trooper, John Smith, talking." Instead I heard, "Hi honey, it's me."

I gave out a blood curdling scream that made Jake recoil two feet. I realized what I had done and I started yelling, "I'm sorry, I'm sorry," to Jake and the telephone."

"Wallie, honey, what's wrong?" Mac screamed.

"Nothing, nothing at all," I answered him. "I think I was having a bad dream. What's wrong with you? You couldn't be home yet."

"No sweetie. We're in a motel in Henrietta, NY just outside of Rochester. It's snowing too hard to go on, and the Highway Patrol Officer told us that the storm has reached Buffalo. We ran into some bad accidents along the way. Most of them were fender benders, but there was at least one fatality. We decided to hole up in a motel. I wish you were Jonathan and he wishes I was Jake, but hey, we'll make the best of it." I could hear the two of them laughing at Mac's bad joke.

"I can't wait to move out of this area. It's New York's Snow Belt, and I've had enough. I'll bet Jonathan will be happy to get home too." I could hear Jonathan yell in the background "But I won't have any snow days." Then they both laughed.

"Is there a restaurant in the motel?" I asked in my best mother hen fashion.

"No, but there's a Denny's up the road. You can see it from the motel, and we can walk to it. Any way we still have the sandwiches Jake made. Driving was so hazardous, we didn't even think of eating."

"Please promise me that you won't continue the trip until it's truly safe. I don't want to have to use the phrase, I love you to death."

"You've given me every reason to stay alive and healthy, so stop worrying. I'll check my plane tickets when I get home and call you with the information. We don't even have to impose on Jake this time. When I booked the trip, I did it with hotel reservations as well. You were still with Marsha then. We're staying at a Holiday Inn near the airport."

"That's fantastic," I said. "We'll finally get our romantic weekend which Marsha so rudely interrupted."

"I can't wait," Mac said. "Let's all get some sleep now. I love you."

"I love you more," I said and hung up the phone.

The next morning it seemed strange to board the commuter train in Oceanside instead of Massapequa, but it seemed like I got into the city in half the time. In fact it was so early, I stopped at a coffee shop and leisurely sipped a coffee and ate a bagel. When I got to the office, the first thing I did was to buzz my boss on the intercom and ask to speak to him.

"Sure," he said. "Come in now. I have to leave in fifteen minutes."

My boss, Izzy Loeffler, is about the best boss anyone could hope for. He worries about the well being of his staff like we were all his kids. Between us staff members we have eight kids and three grandchildren. Izzy never forgets their birthdays, our birthdays or our anniversaries. As much as he loves us and we love him, I have seen the disgust on his face when gay issues have come up in the office. The mention of gay marriage is enough to send him home with apoplexy. The one thing I would not tell him about was my sexual orientation.

"Izzy," I said, "The reason I took yesterday off is that Marsha and I are going to divorce. I'm not living at home, so if you need to get me, please use my cell phone." I started to leave and Izzy grabbed my arm. He is several inches shorter than I. Nevertheless he put his arms around me.

"My boy," he said. "I am so sorry. What can I do? Can I sit with you and your wife and maybe we can straighten things out. This is a terrible thing."

"I appreciate what you are trying to do, but this is for the best. I can't tell you how happy and relieved I am. I do need to look for an apartment, and I was wondering if I could take Friday off."

"Of course, but why wait until Friday? Take tomorrow if it will help."

"Friday will be fine. A friend of mine, who has a good eye, is off that day and he'll help me look. In the meantime I'm staying with another friend, so I'm all set."

"If it has to be, it has to be. It's good there are no children in the equation," Izzy said.

My office routine became normal after that, and nothing untoward happened until Thursday morning. Izzy called me into his office.

"Good morning *boychick*. Are you still handling things all right?"

"You bet, boss. I assure you, I'm really happy."

"Thank God," Izzy said. Izzy always says that looking heavenward, like he and God have a private telephone connection.

"Two things," he said. "I just spoke to your friend Tom Baker in the Buffalo office. He wonders if you could come up there for a couple of days next week. He said you should call him and he'll set the meetings at your convenience.

"The second thing really excites me. I've been trying to transfer that guy to New York for ten years and he always turns me down. Today out of the blue he says to me, if the offer is still open, he's ready to join us sometime this summer. I know you two are good friends. Did he ever give you an inkling?"

"Never! Never! This is fantastic news. I can't wait to call him. Excuse me Izzy." I ran out of Izzy's office and I'm not sure, but I think I heard him mutter, "Sure."

I ran to my office and told my secretary to hold my calls. I closed my door and called Tom on our special inter-office phone system.

Tom picked up the phone. "Baker, here"

"Walters here," I mocked.

"Hey buddy," he said more informally. "What's cooking?"

"Bullshit. What's cooking with you? Izzy just told me the good news. Why didn't you tell me."

"First of all, I couldn't say anything until Izzy approved the transfer, and second of all, I needed to wait for certain things to happen in Dom's life. Izzy just approved me minutes ago so now you know."

"Tell me everything," I begged.

"Well, I never really wanted to transfer, but when you and I became brothers, and then Mac told me he and Jonathan were moving to New York also, I began to look at things differently. Even if I wanted to transfer, I had to think of Dominick. When Mac told us the news, it was Dom who actually broached the subject. He's retiring at the end of the semester and he said let's do it. He has already sent résumés to Brooklyn and Queens Colleges. He told me it would be great to live near New York and the great museums, the opera houses, and the theaters. Besides, we aren't that far from his family here in Buffalo. It's only an hour by plane."

"I hope there's no such thing as too much happiness," I said to Tom. "More and more blessings just keep coming my way."

"God is rewarding you for all your years of misery," Tom said, "and you deserve it. Now how about your next trip to Buffalo? I need you here next week."

"Mac will be here this weekend. I have his arriving flight, but I don't have his departing flight Sunday evening. I'll call him, and as soon as I know it, I'll try to get on his flight. If I do, please set us up for Monday and Tuesday. I'll call you back later today, or tomorrow morning, and we'll firm it up. I love you Tom and you have just made me very, very happy."

"There's a way we can make each other even happier. We'll discuss it when you get here," he said. I knew exactly what he meant. I also knew that Mac was itching for it, and from the way my cock was reacting, I guess I did too. I loved Tom so much, and I really did want to show him just how much.

I called Mac's cell phone. He was at work, and I knew he wouldn't answer it if he was in the middle of an investigation, but I could leave a message. Mac picked up on the first ring.

"Have you got a few minutes?" I asked.

"Yeah sure, you go first and then I have some news for you."

I told him about Tom's transfer and I could almost hear him jump for joy. Then I said that I needed to be in Buffalo next week, and would like to return with him on Sunday, but I needed his flight number. He didn't have it with him, but the plane left from LaGuardia Airport at 7:10 PM and he was on American Airlines. That was enough information for me to try to book that flight.

"What's your big news?" I asked.

"I didn't realize how much vacation time I had. My boss told me to take the days and use the time to pack up my stuff for moving. Today is my last day here on the job. Jonathan is going to help me pack and then I can put everything in storage. I might be able to get to New York days before I start work. I sure hope we can find an apartment this weekend."

"We'll sure try," I said. "I gotta go now before Izzy stops paying me. I love you, detective. Come to me safely and horny on Friday. Ciao."

I got right on the internet and went to American Airlines' web site. I had no trouble booking on Mac's flight and a return on Tuesday evening. I didn't know his seat number, but I was sure we could switch around when we boarded the plane. Then I called Tom back and told him to go ahead with a Monday and Tuesday meeting.

"Monday is sufficient," he told me. "I just figured we'd love to have your company for an extra day. Bye again."

Jake got up early on Friday morning to get to the store. I simply stayed in bed lounging, knowing that I had the day off. I intended spending the day trying to line up apartments for Mac and me to look at, but I didn't have to get up at the crack of dawn.

Jake bent over to kiss me goodbye and as he did, he fondled my package, giving me an instant hardon. I threw a pillow at him and yelled, "Get your sorry ass to work."

"Yes, oh lazy one," he answered.

There was no way I could get back to sleep, so I got out of bed and showered. After I got dressed, I had a lazy spell and decided to have breakfast out. I went to the corner coffee shop and ordered orange juice, scrambled eggs with hash browns, whole wheat toast, and coffee. I bought a morning paper and enjoyed my breakfast and newspaper as if it were a Sunday morning. I was feeling good and enjoying the day. It was mild for this time of year and I breathed in the air and it invigorated me.

I drove to Valley Stream to a Century 21 office and went in. My heart was beating too fast knowing that I was about to set up appointments to rent a love nest for Mac and me.

A lovely woman in her late thirties approached me. She shook my hand, gave me her card, and asked if she could help me. I was glad it was a woman. I intended to tell her that we were a gay couple, and if I got a homophobic male agent, it might not go well at all.

"Yes," I said. "I'm looking for an apartment to rent with my partner. He'll be in town tomorrow and I'd like to set up a few viewings for tomorrow and Sunday, if necessary." Marlene Campbell didn't bat an eyelash.

"How many bedrooms are you looking for?"

"I hadn't thought about it, but I think two would be fine. It would be nice to have a spare bedroom/office for visitors."

"Would you consider looking at condos for rent with an option to buy? In this rotten economy, condo prices have gone into the cellar and they still can't be sold. It's definitely a buyers market."

"That sounds like a plan," I said. "It might really work for us."

We sat at her desk, and she showed me pictures of many apartments, and the price sheets. We zeroed in on five condos with affordable rents and possibly affordable purchase prices. Marlene called the sellers and was able to set up four appointments for the next day. "I'll keep trying to reach the fifth owner," she said. "Can I take you to lunch?" she asked suddenly.

I looked at my watch and could not believe that it was past one o'clock. Mac was arriving at 5:30 and I wanted to start for the airport no later than 4:30.

"I'd love to have lunch with you," I said. She grabbed her purse and coat and took me to a nice little salad bar around the corner.

"I hope you like salads," she said.

"Love them," I fibbed.

At lunch she asked me to tell her about Mac, and I was happy to do so. I showed her his picture and she oohed and aahed.

"He sounds like a winner," she said. "I'm a widow. I live with my teen age son, but he's going to college next September, and it would be nice to have a cop around for protection when I'm alone."

"Yes." I agreed with her. "May, I ask you something?"

"Sure," she said.

"For years I kept my sexual orientation a deep dark secret. Then I met Mac, and now I want to shout how much I love him from the roof tops. You were so OK with it when I told you, that now I wonder at how foolish I might have been."

"Not everyone will react as I have. My son is gay, and he's the most honest, moral person I know. I respect his intelligence and his choices. I support him one hundred percent. You and Mac seem like the kind of persons I would want him to have as friends."

"Thank you," I said and I meant it.

I parked my car in the parking garage and sprinted to the American Airlines terminal. Immediately I checked the incoming flights and Mac's flight was forty-five minutes late. Once more I began to panic. My fears were unfounded and unreasonable, and I vowed to get over it if I had to go to therapy. I couldn't help wishing that our commuting days were over.

To kill time, I had a Danish pastry and a cup of coffee, bought a magazine and waited. My eyes kept darting to the incoming flight monitor and at last, next to his flight, the word, 'LANDED' was flashing. I ran to the gate and too much time passed before the passengers started coming toward me. When Mac spotted me, he started to run.

It reminded me of when Jonathan ran to Jake the day I first met him on the plane. They had kissed each other without caring who saw them or who judged them. I wondered if Mac and I could do that in front of all these people. I didn't have to wait long to find out. Mac grabbed me and kissed me full on the lips. Nobody even paid attention to us. I really had to get over my paranoia.

"We have to go to baggage claim," he said. "I figured I might as well start bringing my things down, so I took advantage of the flight and packed two suitcases full of clothes and stuff. I hope Jake won't mind storing them for awhile."

I drove to the hotel and Mac checked us in. We left the suitcases in the trunk of my car, and brought in his carry on only. I was half undressed before Mac latched the door.

"Hold on, tiger," he said. "I promised Jonathan I'd call him and let him know that I arrived safely. I suggest you call Jake also." We each took out our cell phones and before I was finished talking to Jake, the rest of my clothes lay strewn on the floor, and I was lying prone on the bed. Mac was still talking after I hung up, so I closed my eyes and blissfully waited for him to join me. Suddenly I felt his lips on my cock and then he took me inside him. The moist heat of his tongue and mouth made me forget everything except how much I loved him and how happy I was.

Jake and I had enjoyed each other during the week as had Mac and Jonathan, but nothing compared to how I felt now. I loved my boys in a special way, but I loved Mac with all my body and all my soul. I surrendered myself to him completely, and my body floated into paradise.

At exactly nine o'clock the next morning, we found ourselves entering Marlene's office. I was a bit surprised when she greeted me with a chaste kiss on the lips. I introduced her to Mac. They shook hands but Marlene also planted a kiss on his cheek.

"I hope you don't mind," she said, "but I feel like I know you. Before we head out I'd like you to meet my son. He works here every Saturday. We'll lose him next September when he's off to SUNY Binghamton. He's pre-med," she added proudly.

"Wallie, darling, he's having bullying problems at school about being gay. I won't push him, but I told him that you guys wouldn't mind talking to him, if he wanted to talk to you. Is it all right with you?"

"No sweat," I answered for both of us. "But I have a friend who is a recent high school graduate. He's openly gay and maybe talking to him would be more age appropriate. Let's see how your son feels about it. What's his name?

"Billy!"

She walked us to a back room full of file cabinets. Billy was busy filing away. He stood about 5'9" and weighed about 150 pounds. He had a mop of curly brown hair. His eyes were hazel, and his lips were too thin. He was pleasant looking but far from handsome. When Marlene called his name, he turned to look at us. When he turned, everything changed. There was a light shining from his eyes. I could almost see an aura, a glow, emanating from his body. I felt like God was shining his light on me. I had an unreasonable desire to embrace him and ask him to intercede with God for me. I wondered what Mac was seeing.

Marlene made her introductions and Mac said point blank that it would be an honor to advise him. Billy could not believe that Mac was a tough detective. What kind of job was that for a nice gay boy? We also told him about Jake and Jonathan.

"We won't have time this weekend," I said, "but as soon as Mac and I are settled, we'll all get together and have a good talk."

Mac added, half to Billy, half to himself. "You need some good role models."

Then we left to start our house hunting. Mac grabbed my hand as we got into Marlene's car. He looked as excited as I felt.

Chapter Nine

We went ape over the very first apartment we saw. It was a corner apartment and it was unfurnished. The sellers had been transferred to Chicago. They were already gone and very anxious to sell, or at least to rent. Everything was newly painted and the carpets had just been cleaned. The place was ready to move into.

The second bedroom wasn't the usual small guest room. The apartment actually had two master suites. Both bedrooms were the same size, and each had its own full bathroom. The kitchen was an 'eat-in' kitchen and there was a full size dining room as well. The living room was fairly large and formed an 'L' with the dining room. There was a laundry room off the entrance hall. The apartment was on the fourth floor of an eight story building. There were sliding glass doors in the living room, and in one of the bedrooms. These doors led to a terrace thirty feet long and ten feet wide which could be accessed from either the living room or the bedroom.. The panoramic view from the terrace was breathtaking. The terrace also overlooked the condominium's swimming pool which had been drained for the winter. There was underground parking and each unit owner was assigned two spaces. Also underground was a fully equipped gymnasium.

Mac and I looked at each other and communicated a very positive yes, but just to be polite we went to see the other apartments. By comparison, there was no comparison. We saw three more apartments. The fifth had gone to contract late yesterday afternoon. By the time we had seen all the apartments, it was noon, and we decided to go to lunch.

Over lunch, we discussed the merits of buying versus renting and Mac and I decided to tender an offer to buy. The sellers were asking $195,000 and we offered $180,000. Marlene whipped out her cell phone and reached them in Chicago. They countered with $185,000 and it was a deal.

Back at Marlene's office, we filled out a million papers including a mortgage application with a bank Marlene dealt with. She said that our combined salaries would qualify us for a mortgage on a mansion, but if we could put down a minimum of 20% of the purchase price we could save a half percent on the mortgage rate. We settled on 10% down and the higher rate. Neither of us could come up with $18,500, but we could easily swing $9,250 each.

Marsha had tied up all my assets, so I excused myself a moment, and called Izzy. I explained that I had seen a lovely, appropriate apartment. The sellers were already moved into a new home and were anxious to sell so I got it for a steal, but I needed a down payment of $9,250. Could I borrow it until my assets were unfrozen? I told Izzy I would pay interest at the going rate.

"Interest, shminterest," Izzy said. "Are you sure that's enough? You gotta buy furniture, and maybe curtains and I don't know what else. You should take more."

I started to cry. I wanted to say that my partner had furniture and the apartment had attractive wooden blinds, but I didn't dare. "It's fine." I sobbed. "This will be enough for now and then we'll see. The only problem is I don't know how soon my lawyer can get my assets unfrozen. I hope it will be really soon.

"Don't worry how soon you can pay me back," Izzy said. "I trust you, my boy."

"Thank you, Izzy. I'll see you Monday morning."

I returned to Marlene's office and nodded my go ahead.

"It should take two or three weeks to approve the mortgage and we can close anytime after that," Marlene beamed at us. "All I need is a $1,000 binder."

We each whipped out our check books. Mine was new and this was the first check I wrote on my new, unfrozen account. I had deposited my first pay check into it, and I happily prepared a check to the escrow agent for $500.

Marlene took our two checks and clipped them to our papers. I still had to pay my existing mortgage and household expenses and provide spending money for Marsha until everything was settled. But none of that concerned me. I was happy where I was, and my happiness was worth every penny. What I had thought was impossible, was becoming a reality and worth whatever I had to pay.

"Is it possible to start moving stuff in before the closing?" Mac asked Marlene. I'm almost all packed up in Buffalo and I'd hate to have to go into storage and spend all that extra money."

"That wouldn't be possible, but I'll bet the sellers would let you rent it until then." Out came her cell phone. Once again negotiations began. "How about $200 a week until closing? There will be no security deposit or anything like that. I'll fax them a little informal lease agreement and they'll fax it right back." We both nodded vigorously.

Marlene typed her own version of a lease, and faxed it to Chicago. Minutes later, it was back and signed and she had us sign. She added this to our documents and we each gave her another check for $100 for the first week's rent. She handed us the keys, kissed us both on the cheeks, hugged us both as well, and wished us luck.

"You should call the electric company and the phone company and get services turned on," she suggested. Also at least one of you has to be approved by the condo association before closing. I can set it up at your convenience. It's just a formality."

"It should be me," I said. "I'm the local one. I'll be out of town on business Monday and Tuesday. How about Wednesday or Thursday evening after work?"

I never saw anyone as efficient as Marlene. Again she made a phone call. There was a brief conversation. She told the party on the other end that two young men were buying the apartment jointly. They were both here for the weekend, but one currently lived out of town. The local buyer could meet after work on Wednesday or Thursday. Marlene looked at us and asked if we would like to be interviewed in a half hour. We looked at each other and nodded back at her.

"The president and the vice president will see you in the president's apartment in about thirty minutes. Her name is Joyce Fallon and the vice president is Tony D'Amico. Joyce lives in 7C. Get a move on.

In the car, I told Mac that I was not worried about Joyce, but I was afraid that Tony might be homophobic. Mac said to stop worrying. They couldn't turn us down for sexual orientation. That would be illegal. Our credit was better than what was called for, as Marlene had pointed out. We just had to be our usual charming selves.

Joyce turned out to be a well preserved divorcee in her early thirties. I could see her drooling when she saw us. Tony was a bubbly, overweight Italian gentleman in his sixties. It turned out not to be much of an interview, but more like a let's get acquainted session. They were delighted to hear that Mac was a cop. Everyone thinks that having a cop around adds a measure of protection to the premises. Joyce's interest was piqued when she heard that I was in process of getting a divorce until Tony asked point blank, "Are you two a gay couple?"

I was flabbergasted, but Mac answered proudly, "Yes, we are!" and he took my hand. Joyce looked disappointed, but Tony's reaction surprised me.

"Good," he said in his slightly Italian accent. "The gays in this building are the best owners. They are always doing improvements to their apartments and they are the first to decorate the lobby. You should see how pretty they do the lobby at Christmas. I look forward to you boys moving in. I'll introduce you to the other owners." I was interested to hear that there were other gays in the building.

"We already have the key," I said. "We are renting until the closing so we'll be seeing you around."

"That's wonderful," Tony said. We have to sign off on you, and send a form to Marlene to include with your closing documents. We'll do that right away." He got up and shook both our hands. Joyce did the same and we left.

"It feels like it should be midnight, but it's only 4:00," Mac said.

"I know. Jake gets off at 3 PM on Saturdays. Let's get hold of him and we'll celebrate together tonight. I'll call him to see where he's at."

Jake was home, so we went to his apartment. He was delighted to see Mac again, but made some remarks about how he hated to have to sleep alone tonight. Mac laughed and said that it might not be necessary. "Jonathan asked me to give you one for him. Now what do you think he meant?"

We filled Jake in on our purchase, and told him that after we checked out of the hotel tomorrow morning, we were bringing a load of stuff to the apartment. Then we would have to come back to Jake's place so I could pack a bag before we would head to the airport. Jake said that he would drive us there so that I didn't have to pay for parking overnight for two nights at the airport.

Suddenly I remembered that I had to call the electric company to switch the meter to our name. I called the business office, which fortunately was still open. Since I already had an account in my name, they did not require a security deposit. I opened the account in joint names, and that really excited me. The switch would be made at midnight tonight.

We agreed to hold off with the telephone until Mac moved. We could use our cell phones until then. Eventually we would need a land line to buzz open the lobby door for visitors.

"My family always celebrates big events at Peter Luger's Steak House," Jake said. "Let's go there, but don't even think of taking out a wallet. This is my treat. But first take me to see the apartment. After dinner it would be great if you invited me to play with you at the hotel." He then called the restaurant and made reservations.

We each freshened up before going out to dinner. We had a couple of hours to kill and we chatted excitedly about the marathon day we had just had. "Hey, I gotta call Jonathan," Jake said.

"We should call Tom and Dominick," Mac said.

Two cell phones got busy and there was excited conversations happening on both of them. "We've only been on the market for a week and we've had two offers already," Tom said. "In this slump that's a miracle. We told our agent to accept the second offer, and we are waiting to hear back. I can't believe our luck."

Mac imitated Tony D'Amico. "That's because gays always decorate so pretty," he said.

"Maybe, but now, we have to take a weekend off, and come into New York to look for a place of our own. We appreciate that you bought a condo, but we've lived in a private house for years and I think that's what we'll look for."

"We lucked out with a great real estate agent," Mac noted. "She's so efficient, it's scary. When you know when you are coming in, let Wallie know and he'll set things up for you."

Dinner that night was a culinary delight. I stuffed myself so full, I could only pray that I could make love. Jake took his own car back to the hotel. The kid was really hot to trot and just seeing how eager he was, turned me on. When we entered our room, we double locked the door and drew the curtains. We had to shower individually which was a bit of a bummer. I showered last and by the time I was ready to jump in bed, Mac was down on Jake and Jake was moaning like a banshee.

I approached the bed and Jake turned his head which was nearly at the edge. I offered him my stiffened rod. How moist and warm his mouth felt as it caressed my cock. Mac raised himself off Jake and we all made room on the bed to form a daisy chain. I can't describe the feelings I was experiencing. I loved Mac so much, and I loved Jake as if he was my own son. I still feared my own happiness. I was sure that it would all come tumbling down, and I would be destroyed. At the same time, I mentally kicked myself in the ass for having denied myself so much pleasure for so many years.

We all had enough experience to enable us to control our orgasms, even Jake. As a result we came within seconds of each other. None of us swallowed. Instead, we kissed each other and passed our cum from mouth to mouth in a ritual akin to sharing blood and becoming blood brothers.

When we came up for air, I quipped, "I think this makes us cum brothers."

Jake was still hot to go, but Mac and I needed to rest, so we let Jake fuck both of us, going back and forth. Mac had the pleasure of receiving his cum. That was fine with me. I had been living with Jake since I was thrown out of my house, and his juices were no strangers to my insides. The four of us had stopped using condoms with each other by this time.

Jake left us about midnight. Mac and I cuddled together and fell asleep. In the morning we fucked each other and showered. We cleared out the room and added Mac's carry on bag to his suitcases in the trunk of the car. We checked out and drove to Jake's apartment. His father always covers for him on Sunday, and Jake was still in bed, but he was awake.

"Get dressed," I said, "and we'll take you to breakfast. Then we have a couple of suitcases full of Mac's clothes that we would like to take to the apartment and hang up. By the way, do you happen to have an air mattress?"

"As a matter of fact I do," Jake answered. "It's at the back of the front hall closet."

"Would you mind if I borrowed it? I could take my stuff over too and start living in our apartment."

"Sure," Jake said. "Just as long as we continue having sex and eating dinner together, at least until our men get here."

"You've got a deal," I said. Finally Jake got out of bed sporting a huge morning erection.

"Do you think you guys could do something about this?" he said, pointing to his cock. Mac and I dove right down and took good care of our son.

The three of us packed my meager belongings to take to our apartment, except that I packed an overnight bag for my business trip to Buffalo. We put everything in the car, including the air mattress, and walked to the corner coffee shop, where we had breakfast.

At the apartment, Mac and I hung our jackets, trousers and suits in the master walk-in closet. When I saw our things hanging side by side, the damn tears came again, and both guys put their arms around me. We left shirts, socks and underwear in the suitcases until our furniture would arrive.

We blew up the air mattress and put on the sheet, pillows and coverlet that Jake had given us, and that's where I would be sleeping when I returned from Buffalo on Tuesday night. Jake read my thoughts and said to me, "Look, Dad, You and Mac should break in this place by yourselves. Wallie, leave your car here. I'll take you guys to the airport this evening and I'll pick Wallie up on Tuesday. In the meantime, I'll just leave you guys alone, in your own home, for the very first time."

We kissed him good bye and realized that there was nothing to eat or drink in the house. I would need some staples when I got back on Tuesday. We were just considering going to the supermarket, when there was a knock on the door. We looked at each other as if to say, I wonder who that could be.

Mac opened the door. There stood Tony D'Amico with two gentlemen. I knew immediately that they were one of the gay couples he wanted us to meet. They were both in their early forties, and no taller than 5'9". They both were pleasingly plump, but they had kind and pleasant faces and I liked them immediately. One of them spotted the air mattress on the floor and winked at me.

"This here's Bob, and this one's Robert," Tony said. "They got the same name so that's how we distinguish. And this is Wallie," he pointed at me, "and this big guy is Mac. He's a police detective so watch your p's and q's. I'll leave you guys to get acquainted." He disappeared.

We shook hands all around, and Mac said, "It's a real pleasure to meet you guys. I'd like to offer you something but there's nothing in the house. We were just going to the store to get some basics."

"How about we go with you, orient you to the neighborhood, and then you come to our place for lunch. We can get acquainted over a meal," Bob said.

"Sounds like a plan," I said. "The only thing is we have to watch the time. We have a 7 PM flight to Buffalo and our ride is picking us up at 5:00."

"No sweat," Robert said. "We'll all keep our eyes on the clock for you."

The guys walked us to the nearest super market and we learned that they were both high school math teachers, but in different schools. I was shocked, but I shouldn't have been, to learn that Robert had been married and had two sons in college. His wife was remarried and they were still friends. His sons were cool with his being gay, and they really liked Bob.

We separated while Mac and I bought some staples and Bob and Robert bought a few items which I realized were for lunch. I vowed to reciprocate at the first opportunity. When we got home, we connected the fridge and put our food inside. Then we went to Bob's and Robert's apartment, which turned out to be one floor above, directly over us. They had the exact same apartment we had, and immediately we got some decorating hints and ideas.

After lunch, we all gabbed for about an hour. I knew we were going to be friends, and I told them about Tom and Dom who would be moving down when the semester ended at UB. Then Mac and I asked to be excused. "There's so much to do in the apartment, if I'm to begin using it Tuesday evening," I apologized. We all hugged each other and Mac and I used the stairs to go down a flight to our place. (OUR PLACE, how I loved the sound of it.)

The minute we got into the apartment, we stripped. We wanted to make love as sort of a christening event for the new apartment. We actually found the air mattress to be too uncomfortable for the task at hand, and we ended up making love on the carpeting in our bedroom. After the love making, we tried out the shower. We had been smart enough to buy soap for the sink and the shower, but we had no towels. We laughed at our lack of foresight, but we excused ourselves because we wanted so desperately to use our own apartment that we really hadn't thought beyond our noses..

We dried ourselves with the underwear we had just discarded. I took whatever dirty clothing we had accumulated, and put it into the wash machine. My mind was going a mile a minute, making mental notes of the dozens of things we had to buy.

"Relax," Mac kept saying. "As soon as we unpack my stuff, we'll have everything on your list." It suddenly occurred to me that I was bringing very little into this relationship, and my happiness was suddenly marred.

Of course, by now Mac was adept at reading my face and therefore my mind. "This is a marriage," he said. "Whatever material crap I own, it belongs to you too. If it will make you feel better, I'll let you buy anything we need that I don't have. We'll need furniture for the second bedroom, you know."

I grabbed Mac and I was kissing him like we were parting forever, when Jake came to take us to the airport. We got everything ready to put in the car, which was just my overnight case and Mac's carry on. We left everything in the front hall, and took a moment to go upstairs to say goodbye to Bob and Robert, and introduce Jake to them. We introduced him as our adopted son, and let them know that his partner would be joining him when the semester ended. We chatted for a moment and before we left to get our cases, Bob and Robert hugged and kissed all three of us.

Chapter Ten

We never did get to sit together on the plane. Every seat was taken, but the trip was short. I was seated in the last row just the other side of the galley. A handsome young male flight attendant began to flirt with me unashamedly. He was asking me where I was staying in Buffalo, just as Mac walked back to use one of the rear heads. I pointed at Mac, and told the flight attendant that I would be staying with that handsome hunk.

"Lucky you," he said and walked away.

As we approached the security gates in Buffalo, we both began to look for Jonathan who was supposed to pick us up, but instead we spotted Tom and Dominick, but no Jonathan. The four of us embraced warmly.

"Not that I don't love you guys," I said, "but what happened to Jonathan?" I was very concerned.

"Not to worry," Tom said. "His calculus teacher announced there would be a test the first period tomorrow, and he needed the time to study so he asked us to pick you up. Have you guys eaten dinner?"

"Not yet," Mac answered. "We were going to do fast food on the way home."

"That's what we thought," Dom said. "You'll come home with us. We have dinner ready. You can tell us all about the condo and we'll fill you in on what's happening here."

Of course, we couldn't wait until we got home. The minute we got in the car, Dom told us that their counter-offer had been accepted and the closing was set for May 31. He had an interview scheduled at Brooklyn College for the first Monday of spring break, and another scheduled on Tuesday morning at Queens College. They had booked plane tickets for the Friday afternoon when spring break would begin, and a return flight Sunday evening before school started again. They would be in New York for ten days over the Easter holiday.

"I called Izzy," Tom said, "and he suggested that I could get myself organized at the office and start setting up my schedule while I was there. When I told him that I needed the time for house hunting, he told me in his inimitable way, 'So you'll come into the office in between times.' You gotta love that man. I just wish he wasn't so homophobic."

We arrived at their home and left our two carry-ons in the car. "I just gotta warm the food," Tom said as he rushed into the kitchen. Dom took our coats and settled us on the living room sofa. He poured two glasses of red wine and offered them to us. He poured himself a glass and sat down on a wingback chair and smiled at us.

"I am so happy for both of you," he said, "especially for you Wallie. I know what it's like."

"You do?" I asked. I gathered from Dom's last remark that he had been married also.

"Oh sure," he began to explain. "I got married when I was twenty-one and had a son and a daughter within the first three years. Just like you, Wallie, I knew I was gay when I got married, but I thought I could beat it. Every day, I yearned to be with a man, and every night I fantasized that Rosalie was that man. To say I was miserable would be an understatement. Even the joy I found in my children did not ease the hurt.

"When I was about thirty five, a new teacher, Ken Mervyn, joined the romance language faculty at the university. He was about twenty-eight at the time, and we became instant friends. We had lunch together every day and he began to have dinner at our house every Sunday. Rosie was constantly trying to fix him up, but her efforts were failing.

"Rosie's parents lived in Palermo, Italy, and one summer she took the kids to visit there for six weeks. I knew I would miss the kids, but I also knew that Ken would see to it that I would not be lonely. Looking back on it,

I wonder why I never wondered why he never had a girlfriend. Certainly he was above average in the looks department. It never occurred to me that he might be gay.

"The very first night Rosie and the kids were gone, we had dinner together at Gino's. The night was young and neither of us had summer classes to teach. We literally had all the time in the world.

"'Would you like to go to my favorite hangout?' Ken asked me. "Before you answer, I want to make you aware that it's a gay bar."

He left me speechless. I never had a clue. Since I was staring at him with my mouth open he finally spoke. 'You must certainly have known that I'm gay. I sure don't hide it.'

"'Oh Ken,' I said. 'Of course I'll go to a gay bar with you, but there is something you have to know about me. I'm gay also and I am so in love with you it hurts.'

"We rushed to my car. I had driven that night. The minute we got inside we grabbed each other and began to kiss. He groped at my package and I groped for his.

"'I tried to hint in a million ways how much I love you too," he said, "but you weren't catching on."

"We didn't go to the gay bar that night, but we went to my house, and we made love for three days straight. We never left the house. My ass was so sore, I didn't think I would ever have a normal bowel movement again.

"We continued our secret affair for twelve years, until I was forty-seven years old. My kids got married and had children of their own. Rosie and I had stopped having sex years before that awful day. One evening I told Rosie that Ken and I were going to a hockey game, but, of course, we went to his apartment. We were making love when someone kicked in the door and started taking pictures. I thought we had been so careful, but Rosie had become suspicious.

"My marriage ended, of course. Hallelujah! I moved in with Ken. We had one glorious care free year, before he developed cancer in his liver. He was gone before the whole idea of his illness sunk in. I lived like a hermit for two years after that. My kids and my wife weren't speaking to me and they still don't. I am not allowed to see my grandchildren. They treat me as if I was a pedophile. My grandson would be about seventeen now and a senior in high school. We've never met."

"One evening I decided it was time for me to get out in the world, and I went to Stoney's, the very same gay bar Ken wanted to take me to that first night, and where you two guys met. I sat down at the bar and after a few minutes a handsome young man asked me to dance. I was flattered, and I danced with him. The young man was Tom, and the rest is history."

During Dom's narration, Tom had come in from the kitchen and sat down on the floor at Dom's feet. Everyone was exceptionally silent. Tom stood up and kissed Dom on both cheeks.

"Into the dining room, everybody. Dinner is ready," he said.

This was the happiest dinner I had ever attended. All we could talk about were the vast changes occurring in all our lives, and our hopes and dreams for the future. We all pitched in clearing the table and cleaning up. In no time, the house looked like there had been no mini dinner party.

Once we were settled back in the living room, Tom said, "Wallie, you are familiar with the area where you bought the condo. You'll have to recommend a hotel we can stay at while we are house hunting."

"You have got to be kidding," Mac broke out laughing. "You'll be staying with us. By then our furniture will have arrived and we will have bought furniture for the spare bedroom. It is not open for discussion." I couldn't help noticing that Mac referred to his furniture as our furniture, and I smiled broadly at him.

"That's great, guys," Tom said. "We really appreciate it."

"Nonsense, it will be fun. I can't wait," I said. Then I broke out laughing.

"What's so funny?" Tom asked.

"Well, less than two weeks ago, I would have been desperately trying to make excuses to get away from Marsha so I could be with you guys, and now I'm free as a bird to enjoy all of you." Suddenly my laughter turned to tears and I found myself being hugged by three grown men.

Luckily my cell phone rang and we broke it up. "Hello," I heard Jonathan's voice and a warm glow went through me.

"Hello to you," I said. "How goes the studying?"

"Good, I think. I'll give you a definitive answer tomorrow. Can I come over tomorrow evening?"

"Just a sec," I said. "Jonathan wants to come over tomorrow evening. Are we all doing anything?"

"Tell him to meet us at Gino's at 6 PM and we'll all have dinner together." Dominick said.

"Did you hear that?" I asked Jonathan.

"Yes, and it's a deal. I'll see you then. Ciao."

We talked for a little while longer and then we asked our hosts to drive us home.

"How will you get to the office in the morning?" Tom asked me. "Maybe you guys should stay here tonight. I'll take you to the office tomorrow and Dom can drive Mac home to continue packing."

"That's a good idea," Dominick said. "I only have one morning class tomorrow. Then we can go back to your place, and I'll help you pack. Now that you have a place in New York, I'll bet you're anxious to finish up."

"Yes, I am anxious, as a matter of fact. By the way, the condo is in Valley Stream. Technically we will be living in a suburb of New York. Valley Stream is the city I'll be working for. It's an easy ride to either Brooklyn College or Queens College and a short commute to New York. I would recommend that you look for a house there or close by. We'd want you to be near us and Jake and Jonathan. They live in Oceanside, which is only a stone's throw away."

Mac went out to Tom's car and got our two carry on bags. Dom showed us to the guest bedroom and bath while Tom secured the house for the night. "There are plenty of towels and wash cloths in the closet in the guest bathroom," Dom advised. "Please don't be shy with us. Tom and I sleep nude and walk around the house that way, once we have drawn the blinds, that is."

"That's fine with us," Mac said. "We do the same."

Mac and I undressed. We were grungy from the airplane trip and from the hectic day we had before Jake drove us to the airport, so we headed for the shower. We showered together and of course we got ourselves worked up into a sexual frenzy. Once we were all dried up, we opened the door and headed for the bedroom, both sporting erections. Imagine our shock to find Tom and Dom sitting on our bed totally naked. They stood up as we entered and they were both hard as nails also. Dom is 6' 3" tall, and his erect cock is at least eight hard inches. Tom was not so well endowed, somewhere around six inches. Still, he had a lean, muscular body, and I was immediately turned on by both of them.

"We want to bond with you sexually," Tom said.

"We want to express how much we love you, my brothers," Dominick added.

"If you don't mind," I said. "Over the year's I have fantasized making love to Tom a thousand times. I'd like my dream to come true tonight."

"It's true for me too," Tom said. He took my hand and led me to the master bedroom. As we left the guest room, Dom approached Mac and began to kiss him while he drove his cock against Mac's body. The last thing I heard was Mac moaning. They never did bother to close the door. For that matter, neither did we.

Tom and I lay down on his bed and immediately wrapped our arms around each other, and ground our cocks together.

"I have a confession to make," I said. "I used to check you out in the men's room so I knew just what to expect tonight."

"You fucking pervert," Tom laughed. "I used to do the same to you. What do you want to do to me on this miraculous occasion?"

"Everything," I answered. I turned Tom on his back and began to explore his body with my tongue. I used Mac's technique for a trip around the world and I was thrilled when I heard Tom's moans, his sighs and his little whines. Tom was enjoying himself and that made me so happy. I took my sweet time and finally I went down on him. The minute I did, he came. That's how excited I had gotten him.

He lay immobile for a little while and then he said, "Shit!"

"What's the problem?" I asked.

"I wanted to fuck you."

"Relax love, we have tomorrow night and all day Tuesday, and way into the future." Then it was my turn to say 'shit.'

"What?" Tom asked.

"Jonathan! He'll expect some action tomorrow and we owe it to him."

"Not to worry, Bro. There's always room for one more," Tom answered philosophically. Then he turned me on my back and went down on me without preliminaries. When he came up for air for a moment, he said, "I can do better, but it's getting very late."

There was something in the way he peeled back my foreskin with his lips that set me over the edge way too soon. Afterwards we fell asleep in each other's arms.

In the other room, Mac was first to apply his magical sex technique on Dom. Poor Dom came long before Mac even put his lips to Dom's cock. Nevertheless Mac kept on enjoying his trip around the world, Dom's world, and after sucking Dom's cock for a little while, Dom came again. I was to learn later, as Mac had just learned, that Dom's cum was sweet and not at all salty. We wondered if that happened as we aged.

I guess because neither of these two guys had to go to work early the next day, they took the time to enjoy each other equally. Dom greased his ass and handed the lube to Mac who greased his cock. Dom lay on his back and raised his legs. Mac straddled him and Dom wrapped his legs around Mac's waist urging him to enter him. You don't have to tell Mac anything twice. He placed his cock on Dom's opening and started to enter slowly. To his surprise he slid right in. He was astonished. Everyone else he had ever been with, including me, offered some measure of resistance. That is not to say that Dom wasn't tight. He was very tight, but his sphincter offered no resistance. Mac thought, 'I guess that comes from years of practice.'

When Mac came, he gushed up Dom's ass, and some of his cum dribbled out. To Mac's surprise, Dom scooped it up with his forefinger and swallowed it.

The next morning, at the marketing conference with our clients, Tom kept kneeing me under the table. It was all I could do to concentrate, and I kept giving him stern warnings with my eyes. Thank God for the passage of time, no matter how slow. The meeting finally ended at 5:30 and the clients departed. Tom rushed me into his office and locked the door. He grabbed me and my package and began kissing me.

"I'm so happy, I'm so happy," he kept repeating. "I have Dom and now I have you and Mac. All my wildest dreams have come true." His voice cracked.

"I love you too," I said. "You were my major fantasy, and now we will have each other and our partners forever. But this is not the time or the place. Let's freshen up so we can meet the guys at Gino's."

Jonathan was already there when we arrived, but Mac and Dom were not. We greeted each other with hugs and kisses. When we separated, Jonathan looked back and forth into our faces. After awhile he said, "Aha! You two have had sex together, haven't you?"

"For Christ's sake, Sherlock. How did you know?"

"There's a glow I can see in people's eyes when they have made love to someone they really love and it's not just sex. You two have the glow."

"I can see we'll never be able to hide anything from you," Tom said. Just then Mac and Dom came in, and Jonathan said, "Uhoh! They've got the glow also. You guys better not leave Jake and me out of your lives. We love you too."

"That will never happen," I assured my son, "and I'll prove it to you tonight."

"Do we really need to eat dinner?" Jonathan asked jokingly. "Why can't we go straight home?"

A meal is not just the food served. It is enhanced by the presentation and the service, of course. But that still doesn't make it perfect. Perfection comes with the people you break bread with. Except that Jake was not with us, I was surrounded by the people I loved most in the world. As long as they were at my side, I knew I was safe. Absolutely nothing in the world could harm me. That's what made this meal the perfect meal, the most perfect I have ever eaten.

"I have news for you, honey," Mac said to me. "With Dominick's help, I have finished packing. I can't even stay in my apartment any longer. First thing tomorrow, I'll arrange for the mover to come. In the meantime, Dom said I could stay with them." He looked at Jonathan. "And yes, young son, you can come over whenever you feel horny, which is all the time." Jonathan blushed and we all laughed.

We knew that tonight we would switch partners from the night before. But what about Jonathan? As if in answer to what I was wondering, he asked. "Would it be all right if I teamed with Dominick and whoever he's with tonight? I swear I have never been with such a tall guy, and something tells me he is proportionate all over."

"How right you are," Tom commented. "And we would never deny you the pleasure." So that's how Dom, Jonathan and I ended up a threesome that night, and Tom and Mac were left alone to get better acquainted.

Dom, Jonathan and I were particularly inventive in our love making. I don't think we missed a trick learned from years of viewing three ways in porn films. Jonathan begged Dom to fuck him. He wanted that huge drilling tool up his ass desperately. Dom was hesitant, afraid he would hurt the boy, but Jonathan was not about to be deterred.

It took a lot of grease, patience and hard work, but Dom finally inserted his full size and girth up Jonathan's pleading ass. When Dom's beauty was fully up there, and all that was visible were his balls, Jonathan began to scream, "Thank you God. This is what I was born to do. Now fuck me and fuck me hard," he instructed Dominick. I remembered that Jake had said the same thing to me the day he gave me that blessed hickey.

It confirmed what I had known all along. Jake and Jonathan were meant for each other, and AMEN! to that. All the while I was thinking that thought, I was happily rimming Dominick's ass.

Chapter Eleven

Jonathan went back to his dorm room about 10:30 PM. After he left, Tom, Dominick, Mac and I went downstairs into the kitchen where Dom made us cappuccino. Tom found some biscotti in the pantry, and we had ourselves a mini feast. We talked and talked about our plans for the future. Did I mention that we were all naked?

While everyone was busy talking, I began to reflect on my former "wannabee" life. A mere few weeks ago, I could not have conceived of an evening like this. I would have been watching, but not absorbing, some idiotic television show. I would be in my easy chair and Marsha would be on the sofa with her legs up. She too would be staring at the inane image in front of us, and I now wondered how much she was absorbing. Maybe she was dreaming of her "wannabee" life, just like I was.

Now here I was, sitting naked with my three best friends, engaged in an animated conversation, planning our futures. I was so happy, my whole body felt electrified. Then every so often, I would experience that feeling of dread. This is the life I had dreamed about and yearned for my whole life, at least since puberty. Now it was real, and too good to be true. Something bad was going to happen, I just knew it. I could feel it in my bones. I told myself that my dreadful fears were unfounded and unreasonable, and I would have to get over it.

"Are you all right, kiddo?" I heard Mac ask me. I was roused from my reverie and looked up to see three concerned faces staring at me.

"I'm fine," I said. It's just that I can't seem to accept my good fortune. I'm so happy it scares me. Please just bear with me until it all sinks in."

That lightened the mood. Someone made a joke about our cocks going into shrinking mode, which set us off in gales of laughter as we cleaned the kitchen. The four of us went upstairs. We kissed each other goodnight in the hallway and went to sleep; Mac and I in the guest room, and Tom and Dominick in their own bedroom.

Mac and I slept late, but in some semi conscious state, I could hear Tom and Dom getting ready for work. I wanted to get up, but I was too woozy. Besides Mac was wrapped around me and he's a pretty big fellow. Indeed when we did wake and go downstairs, our brothers were gone. We found a note on the kitchen table instructing us where we could find everything.

I called Tom at the office to see if I was needed for anything, but he told me to just enjoy the time I had left with Mac. While I was talking to Tom, Mac was perusing the yellow pages. He waited for me to get off the phone, and he made his first call to a mover. In all, he made three calls. He told each one how many boxes there were to be moved and the dimensions of the boxes, which were all the same size. He also described every piece of furniture. With all that information, each of them quoted on the phone. The costs ranged from $1,950 to $2,375 with insurance. The middle price was $2,100 and Mac decided to go with that mover because he had a good reputation.

Mac called him back and asked when he could make the move. The gentleman told him the earliest would be next Tuesday, a week from today. Mac said that he would pay an extra $500 if he could pick up the load this week and deliver by the weekend. The mover put him on hold and when he returned, he said, "OK, Mr. MacNeal, we can pick up tomorrow and deliver on Friday morning. I'll bring the contracts with me tomorrow. I own the business and I haven't personally done a haul in a few years, but my son and I will be doing it ourselves." Mac gave him his address in Eggertsville and he said he would be there at 8 AM.

Next Mac called American Airlines and booked a one way ticket on a plane leaving at 5:15 PM tomorrow. My heart began skipping beats. From tomorrow night on, Mac and I would be together forever. Then it came over me again, that unreasonable dread. What was the matter with me?

Mac didn't have to take me to the airport until 4 PM, and Jake would be there to pick me up. You would think that we would spend the day making love, but we took a break. First we went to Mac's apartment to make sure that nothing was forgotten. Then we had a nice lunch in a neighborhood restaurant. After lunch we went back to Tom's house, sat on the sofa holding hands, and watching soap operas.

When my plane arrived in New York, I really wanted to go to 'our' place, but Jake begged me to spend the night with him. With all of us in Buffalo these past few days he had been especially lonely, and now his horniness had reached a critical point. I laughed when he told me this, and I agreed to spend the night with him.

Jake made us a light dinner, and after dinner we stripped and showered together. We lingered long in the shower, playing and teasing each other. Jake kept soaping my cock over and over again and with his other hand he was soaping his ass. Finally he was satisfied and begged me to fuck him.

"Only if you fuck me first," I said. "You're much hornier than I am. I'm all done out. If I'm lucky, I'll get hard enough to fuck you. I'm hoping that when you fuck me that will do it for me. If not, you'll have to settle for a blow job."

"I can live with that," he said, and he began to soap his cock while I did my ass. I turned my back to him and he entered me easily. I guess I was getting all stretched out. He was truly horny. He came in four or five strokes. How good my ass felt with his hot jism filling it up.

"Look," he said pointing at my cock. It was hard as a ramrod and I made an easy entry into my son's luscious, bubbly ass. It took me considerably longer to cum. I was thrusting as hard as I could, but Jake kept yelling, "Harder, harder, please." All I could think of was that this would have been more comfortable in bed than in the shower. At last I felt my climax approaching. I pumped harder, and still Jake yelled, "Harder!"

Afterwards, we rewashed our sweaty bodies, dried off, and climbed into bed. I called Mac on my cell phone and Jake called Jonathan on his land phone. Both conversations were pretty much the same as we told our guys how much we loved them. "I can't wait to pick you up at the airport tomorrow evening," I told Mac. "We'll never be apart again."

"Not true," Mac laughed. "You'll have your damned business trips, and I'll have to settle for Tom, Dom, Jake or Jonathan." At first I didn't realize that he was pulling my leg until he burst out laughing.

"Very funny!" I quipped.

"Go back to fucking Jake," he said, "but save enough for me for tomorrow."

"I promise."

The next day, reality hit me. At about 10:00 AM I was served with divorce papers. I glanced through them. Marsha wanted everything including my testicles. I called my brother-in-law who said that I should come over at lunch time. His office was within walking distance of mine. In fact, we often had lunch together.

When I got there, Allen sent out for lunch for the two of us. While we waited he read the divorce papers.

"She doesn't want much, does she?" he joked. "OK so what's the real reason for your split? You used homosexuality as an excuse, didn't you?"

I broke out laughing. "Listen, Al," I said. I love you like you were my real brother, and I hope this won't impact on our relationship, but the truth is I have been gay all my life. I thought I could kick it by getting married, but I found out it's not something you can wash away in the shower." I took out the picture of Mac that was getting worn out in my wallet.

"This is Mac, Cornelius MacNeal. We are in a committed relationship. He's moving from Buffalo to be with me. He'll be starting as a detective with the Valley Stream police department two weeks from Monday, and he's arriving permanently this evening."

"Your Mac is very good looking. I swear, Wallie, It makes no difference to me who you sleep with. I love you man. Besides I never really thought you and Marsha gelled. You and Mac can stay with us until you find a place."

I started to laugh. "Allen, we bought a condo in Valley Stream. We're renting it until the closing in about three weeks. Mac's furniture is arriving sometime on Friday. I reached into my briefcase and brought out the folder Marlene had given us. Here's the contract of sale. You can review it for us, please.

"Now here's the story. I don't want to fight Marsha, but she has tied up every asset I have. I don't care. It's worth it to be free of her. But my 401K plan is mine, and I need to borrow from it to make my down payment. Izzy is lending me the money until then. Can you get my 401K released quickly? It's all I want from her."

"Yes, I can, but I'm pretty insulted," Allen said. "We're family. You should have come to me. I would have lent you the money. I'm also pissed to learn about Mac, and the apartment and the fact that you didn't confide in us."

"In a way, Izzy is family too. Besides as soon as you get me access to my 401K, I'll pay him back. As for the other stuff, frankly I was worried how you would take it. I was afraid you would reject me."

"OK guy," he said. "You're a jerk, but I love you, and you owe me. Mac is coming in this evening. We'll give him tonight to get back his land legs and you two are coming for dinner tomorrow evening. That's not open for discussion. Jenna and I will want to meet him, and you haven't been around to see your two fast growing nephews in weeks. Don't you want Mac to meet your family, or are you ashamed of us?"

"Of course, I want him to meet you all. Is six about right?"

"Perfect." He grabbed me and gave me a big hug. Once again I had to wonder what bogey man I had been afraid of all these years.

Mac's flight was scheduled to arrive at 6:25 PM. I hadn't used the railroad to get into town today. I had driven, and my car was parked, at great expense, in a nearby parking ramp. I left the office at 5:00, allowing for rush hour traffic and I headed for LaGuardia. For a change I had no difficulty finding a parking space. At this hour most cars were leaving the parking facility, not coming in.

Once in the terminal, I checked the incoming flight monitor. Mac's plane was on time. I looked at my watch. I had about forty minutes to wait. My pulse was racing and I needed to calm down. I found a coffee shop and ordered coffee and a cinnamon roll. Whenever I am nervous, I crave sweets. I vowed to watch myself. I didn't want to get fat and lose Mac, even though he told me that he would love me no matter what.

By the time I finished my coffee, the monitor read "LANDED" next to his flight. I flew to the security area and waited for him. He was one of the last off the plane and again that terrible feeling of dread came over me, but when I saw him, the cloud lifted.

He embraced me, but we didn't kiss. We just stood there for what seemed like hours, just hugging. It wasn't hours, but it must have been a long time because the flight crew was coming out of the secured area. One of them tapped Mac on the shoulder. I looked up. It was the flight attendant who had flirted with me last week.

"Hey, you two," he said. "Call me." He handed Mac his card. At least it broke us up and we headed for baggage claim. Mac had brought another two suitcases full of clothes, which he didn't put on the moving truck.

Once we were in the car, I had a crazy thought. "Mac, honey, how are you going to get your car down here?"

"Wallie, I drove an unmarked police vehicle. I had to turn it in. I'll be getting another one here too, as soon as I get started. We'll have to get along with one car until then."

"You might have noticed," I pointed out, "I worry a lot."

"That you do sweetheart. That you do."

"Mac, do you realize that we are driving home together, our home."

"Yes," Mac answered. "Isn't it wonderful?"

I stopped at a diner that was near our apartment and we had dinner. From there we called Jake and Jonathan, and Tom and Dominick. Everyone was thrilled that Mac had arrived safely, and we were about to start our lives together. Suddenly, that all too familiar feeling of dread came over me, but this time the feeling was valid. How could I hide my relationship with Mac from Izzy? How could Tom hide Dominick from him? Would Izzy fire both of us? Izzy was the closest thing to a father I had. My own Mom and Dad were killed in a car crash shortly before I married Marsha.

I determined not to let Mac know what I was thinking. He was so much braver than I. When he interviewed for his job, he laid his sexual orientation right out there on the table, and he got a 'so what' attitude for his efforts. All I could hope for was that Izzy loved Tom and me enough to be understanding, and to discard his prejudices. I prayed that if people close to him were gay, instead of some abstract queers, he might have a change of heart. Was it wishful thinking? I hoped not.

I pulled into the underground parking lot and into one of our assigned spaces. I popped the trunk and each of us took one of Mac's suitcases. On the elevator going up, it took all my effort not to cry. Mac, of course, sensed what was going on with me and said, "Hang on old boy. Hang on."

"Let me," Mac said and he unlocked our door.

"Home sweet home," I said as we walked in. Mac closed the door. We dropped both suitcases and fell into each other's arms. "I love you so much," I said.

"I love you more than that," Mac said.

"Let's hang up your stuff," I suggested. "I put wine, crackers, and cheese in the fridge, and I bought some plastic cups. Let's drink to our new home, and then you can use me to fuck your brains out," I said. We went into the bedroom and Mac started unpacking. While he was hanging his clothes in the closet, I told him about the divorce papers and our command dinner invitation for tomorrow evening. I was afraid that he would object, and I was pleasantly surprised to hear him say, "That's fantastic. I can't wait to meet your family."

If the shoe was on the other foot, I'd be scared shitless. I'd be sure they would spend the evening judging me, and blaming me for making Mac gay. I clearly had more paranoia to overcome than I first imagined.

"I have a new, unattached credit card," I informed Mac. "Let's buy a guest bedroom suite on Saturday, and get the room ready for our two distinguished visitors."

"We should make a to-do list," Mac said. He went to his suitcase which still contained his socks, shirts, and underwear. From the side pocket he pulled out a pad and a pencil. We sat on the carpeted floor, leaning against the wall. Mac began to write"

Thursday:

1) Arrange for land line telephone service.
2) Buy a kitchen and two bedroom phones. "Wait a minute," he said, and he ran out to the terrace. In a second he returned and added to number 2.
2) Buy a kitchen, two bedrooms and a terrace phone.
3) Do a big food shopping and buy more than the basic food stuffs.
4) Walk the neighborhood, and check out the amenities
5) Give Wallie a great big kiss when he gets home from work.
6) Have dinner with Jenna, Allen, Allen,Jr., and Sammy.
7) Make love to Wallie.

"Can you think of any thing else?" he asked. I shook my head. "I'll work on Friday's list during the day tomorrow."

"Drive me to the train station tomorrow morning, and you'll have the car if you need it," I suggested.

"I can't think of anything more domestic than to drive you to the train station. It will be my pleasure," Mac said.

I picked up the food, and placed it back in the refrigerator. We had enough foresight to buy a box of garbage bags and that's where we threw the dirty plastic glasses. When that was done, Mac unceremoniously stripped in the kitchen and so I did the same. He led me into the bathroom and turned the taps in the shower. When the water temperature was satisfactory to both of us, we began a ritual which was to become our standard foreplay.

We each, in turn, soaped each other's bodies. We did this slowly and sensuously. We especially massaged our cocks with plenty of soap suds and concentrated on our ass holes. We both loved rimming and we wanted that area to be particularly clean. Occasionally we would rinse each other off and we would alternately suck our cocks or rim our ass holes. In short we did whatever we could to work ourselves into a sexual frenzy. Then, if we had been able to keep from cumming, we would dry each other off, get into bed and suck and fuck for as long as we could. Of course, tonight we were to use the floor and we were grateful that it was thickly carpeted.

We had not only bought food staples on the day we took possession, but bathroom staples as well, so fortunately we had plenty of lube. We lay down on the plush carpeting and wrapped into each other. Mac's tongue tried to play deep throat with me, but eventually the tips of our tongues began to play and tickle each other.

Mac rolled over on top of me and began his game of taking me around the world with his tongue. When his tongue went up my ass, I screamed, "Enough! Please suck me or fuck me. I've got to cum."

He took me into his mouth and I began to cry. Mac was bringing me to ecstasy and I could barely tolerate the joy. His tongue was swathing all around my head and the shaft, and I screamed out loudly as I came, spurting gusher after gusher into his mouth. When I could breathe again, I screamed out. "Mac, I love you so much. Don't let anything happen to you. I would die if you got hurt."

"Hush," he whispered. "Nothing is going to happen to either of us. We're going to have a long and happy life."

For the first time, I almost believed him.

Chapter Twelve

The next morning found us waiting for the elevator to the underground parking. As agreed, Mac was going to drive me to the train station, and have use of the car all day. When the elevator door opened, there stood Bob and Robert.

"Hey guys," Bob almost yelled, "are you all moved in yet?"

"We are, but our furniture isn't due in until tomorrow morning," Mac replied.

"If you aren't set up yet, you're more than welcome to have dinner with us tonight," Robert extended an invitation.

"Thanks guys, we really appreciate the invitation," I said, "but we are having dinner at my sister's home tonight. She lives in Fresh Meadows."

"Well welcome home anyway, and maybe we can do something together over the weekend. If you like vintage films, there's a couple of classics showing at The Thalia this weekend." I knew that The Thalia was a Manhattan movie house that showed artsy-fartsy films.

"Thanks," I said, "but I expect we'll be busy unpacking and setting up all weekend. It sounds great, however, and we'd like to take a rain check."

"Sure. No problem," Bob said, as they headed to separate parking spaces. "See you around." They both gave us a friendly wave good bye.

Getting served with divorce papers in the office yesterday should have been enough trauma for the whole month. What happened this morning sent me into a tailspin, from which I could only recover using all my strength. The minute I got into the office, Izzy was there to pounce on me.

"Please Wallie," he said. "Can you come into my office. I gotta speak to you in private."

"Sure," I said. There it was, that dreadful feeling. I was convinced that Izzy found out about me, and I was about to be fired.

Izzy not only closed his office door, he locked it. Then he buzzed his secretary and told her that we were not to be disturbed.

I was really worried now and I blurted out, "Izzy what is it? What's wrong? You're scaring me." He sat down at his desk and motioned for me to occupy a chair facing him. "Tell me!" I begged.

"You know I have a daughter. She's my only child. She married a career army officer almost twenty years ago. He was a great guy and he treated my daughter like a princess. They had one child, a son. Wallie, I tell you, my grandson is a brilliant scholar, and such a good person. Anyway, my son in law was killed in Iraq two year's ago. He was not of my faith, but we buried him with full military honors in a good Christian burial." Izzy started to cry. "I'm sorry," he said. "I loved that man so much."

"Last night my daughter and my grandson came to dinner. My Gloria made a real feast. During dinner, we were all telling jokes and in general we were having a good time. Then I started to tell an innocent little joke. I meant nothing by it, I swear." Izzy hesitated.

"What was the joke about?" I ventured to ask.

"It was a little derogatory."

"Derogatory to whom?" I was determined to make Izzy spit it out.

"Well, it was about fairies. I was making fun of them. It was just in fun. You gotta have a sense of humor."

"I take it someone at the table was offended," I offered.

"Yeah," Izzy sighed, "my grandson."

"Was he mad because he doesn't like to see anyone being slurred, or was he mad because he's gay?" I really wanted to know.

"My grandson jumped up and in a really sweet voice, a soft voice, he said to me, 'Grandpa there is something I have to tell you. I swore I would tell you before I left for college, but I have been so scared. Now you have to know the truth. I'm seventeen, almost eighteen. I'm going to college in the fall. I don't want to hide who I am from anyone anymore. I'm gay and that's never going to change. I'm still me. You loved me a minute ago. I hope you can love me even now, because I love you more than I can ever tell you in words.'"

I remained silent so Izzy continued.

"He looked at me and I swear Wallie, a light shone out of his eyes. His body was enveloped in an aura like an angel. I felt like God was looking at me and maybe judging me. I grabbed him and hugged him and we both cried together for a long time.

"I assured him over and over that I loved him, and that nothing could change that. While I was holding him and he was sobbing on my shoulder, I had an epiphany. I realized that if anyone would hurt this boy, or poke fun at him, I would be capable of bringing harm to that person. I thought of all the times I had made derogatory statements about gays when I didn't even know them. I was ashamed, and I asked Billy to forgive me. He couldn't understand why I was asking for forgiveness."

Billy!! A light shining from his eyes! An aura enveloping his body. I had seen a boy like that. Could this Billy be Marlene's son? Could she be Izzy's daughter?

"Izzy," I asked, "what's your daughter's name?"

"Marlene. Why do you ask?"

"No reason." I said. "Why did you tell me all this and why did you lock the door?" I thought my questions were reasonable.

"Billy told me that he had nobody to help him through this, and then I thought of someone who could help," Izzy said. My heart skipped more than one beat.

"Who?" I asked innocently.

"Your friend in Buffalo, Tom Baker. He's coming down soon. Do you think you could ask him to have a little talk with Billy, or even a long talk?"

"You think Tom is gay?" I asked. I was truly shocked, not because Izzy outed him to me, but that Izzy knew that he was gay.

"Sure," Izzy assured me. "Everybody knows. Don't tell me you don't know."

"I can honestly answer that I didn't know. How does everyone know but me. I'm his friend." The fact is I really didn't know until I heard Dom's voice by accident.

"How long have you known and how did you find out?" I had to know.

"He was in New York on business one time. I can't remember when it was, maybe four or five year's ago. Anyway, I knew he was a bachelor, but he kept talking about a house 'we' were buying or about a place 'we' went to visit, and so on, so I figured the other half of 'we' was not a woman."

"Did it change how you felt about him?"

"Funny thing. It didn't matter to me at all. I love Tom like I love you; like I love Billy," he said. I let it slide that he put me in with Billy and Tom.

"Wow!" I said. "I'm speechless. I know Tom, and I am sure he'll be happy to speak to your grandson."

"You'll talk to him, then," Izzy sighed. Thank you my boy."

I ran back to my office and closed the door. I decided to lock it also. The first call I made was to Marlene. "Can you give me a minute?" I asked. "I just talked to your father, Izzy Loeffler, about Billy. Surely when you took my employment history, you must have realized that I worked for him. Why didn't you say something?"

"I was afraid you would out Billy. We both felt that he should tell my father himself and in his own way. Did you tell him about yourself?"

"No, not yet. But I intend to tell him today. He outed my friend Tom to me. I told him I didn't know that Tom was gay. That was the truth until a few days ago, but Tom is scared to death that Izzy will find out. I've got to call him and relieve his anxiety, and then I'm going to take Izzy to lunch and tell him about me."

"I know my father," Marlene said, "and for all his bluster, he'll still love you."

My next call was on the inter office phone. I shook as I heard Tom. "Baker, here," he said.

"I know it's you," I said curtly. "I dialed your private number. Don't talk and don't interrupt. I've got something unbelievable to tell you." I told Tom what had transpired just moments ago, and there was stunned silence at the other end. "Tom," are you still with me?" I asked.

"Yes, yes. Do you know how relieved I am? I don't have to hide my identity at work anymore. I can talk about Dominic freely and Izzy has the heart I always knew he had. You don't have to tell him how happy I'll be to talk to Billy. I'm going to call him myself."

"When you do call him," I said, "as far as Izzy knows I just found out about you today. Let me transfer your call to him right now."

After I transferred the call, my phone showed a red light indicating it was in use. I waited until the light went out and I hurried to Izzy's office. After he told me to come in, I asked if we could have lunch together because I wanted to speak to him about Billy, Tom and other matters. I threw Billy in because I figured he wouldn't turn down an invitation to talk about his grandson.

"Sure," he said. "That will be lovely.

At lunch, I started the ball rolling by asking Izzy if he believed in the theory of six degrees of separation.

"Are you kidding?" he asked me. "In my experience it's more like three degrees. Why? You got a small world story for me?"

"Wait until you hear," I said. "The real estate agent who is handling the purchase of my house is your daughter, Marlene. May I say we hit it off right away and became friends, not just business associates. She introduced me to Billy. When I looked at him, I saw his aura that you were talking about. There is something spiritual about that boy. You can tell he's going to do great things, and that people will always trust and follow him."

"You saw it too?" Izzy asked with a tear in his eye.

"When I found out that you were talking about Billy and Marlene, my first call was to her, not to Tom Baker. She knew who I worked for, and I asked her why she didn't say anything. She told me that she was afraid that I would out Billy, and she didn't want that to happen. She wanted Billy to tell you himself."

"Yes," Izzy said. "I'm glad the boy did. How did it come about that Marlene and Billy told you that he was gay?"

I had maneuvered the conversation to this exact moment. I took Mac's ever fraying photo from my wallet, and vowed to get a real photo, not a computer print out to show people. I unfolded the picture and laid it out in front of Izzy. Mac was smiling back at Izzy with his private area covered by a book.

"So," Izzy said, "I see a very handsome man with a terrific body, but it's a kind of dirty picture. Why are you showing it to me?"

"The guy's name is Cornelius MacNeal, Mac for short. Izzy, you're not only my boss, you're a dear friend. Since my dad died, I think of you as my father so please hear me out. Mac and I bought the apartment together. We are life partners. I'm gay also."

Well of course I left Izzy speechless. After awhile he said, "Oy! You got any more surprises for me today? How much more can this old heart of mine take? I guess Marlene and Billy know."

"Yes. It was Marlene who asked us to mentor Billy. She wants him to have positive role models. That's how I knew he was gay and why she didn't tell me she was your daughter. The crazy thing is that I really didn't know about Tom and he didn't know about me. We just found out, which will probably bring us even closer."

"Whew, well let's hear about your Mac. I want to know all about him. If you're like a son to me, I suppose he is too."

"I met Mac in Buffalo, and we pretty much fell in love at first sight." Izzy cringed when I said that, but he didn't say anything. It was going to take a lot for him to accept all this.

"When I was robbed in my hotel room, imagine my surprise to find that Mac was the detective on the case. I had never even asked what he did for a living. Anyway, after my split with Marsha, we were free to be together. He has moved down here, and he starts with the Valley Stream police department a week from Monday. His moving truck will be here tomorrow. I can't wait for you to meet him."

Izzy graciously said, "I can't wait to meet him also. A policeman, yet. That will be a real good role model for Billy."

"Would you like to hear about Tom's partner?" I asked with a gleam in my eye.

"Why not? Let me get it all at once so it can all sink in."

Again Izzy's eyebrows raised in appreciation when he heard that Dom was a college professor. Izzy had had very little formal education. He was a self made man in every sense of the word. The bottom line was that his respect for educated people far exceeded what that accomplishment was actually worth in many of them.

"This man, I can't wait to meet, either," he said.

When the check came, I argued with Izzy. I insisted that I had invited him to lunch and I should pay. "Your money has a foul odor. It stinks here," he said, "so put it back in your wallet where it won't smell so bad."

When we stood up to leave, Izzy gave me a hug. "You and Tom and your partners are wonderful role models for Billy. I'm glad he has you. When Tom and Dominick get here, I'm inviting everyone to dinner, so I can meet everybody. Gloria cooks better than any chef in a restaurant."

Back in the office, I called Marlene and filled her in. "See," she said. "I told you so. My father is a big bear, with a big roar, but an even bigger heart. My late husband, Edward adored him. My dad took his death really hard. I know he's not over it yet."

The rest of the day seemed to drag on forever, but finally I was rushing to Penn Station to grab my commuter train. Once I was seated, I called Mac and told him what time the train would arrive in Valley Stream.

"Every day is an adventure," I said. "Wait until you hear today's news." I hung up immediately so he wouldn't bug me to tell him. This news needed savoring over dinner.

Mac was waiting for me at the train station just as Marsha used to do. I hopped into the passenger seat and gave Mac a peck on the cheek.

"What's the big news?" he asked.

"Later," I said, "over dinner. "It's complicated and I want to get it exactly as it happened. This way my sister and Allen can get the news at the same time."

We went home where I freshened up, and dressed down. Then off we went to my sister's house. Her older boy, Allen, Jr., aged seven, answered the door. He leaped into my arms. "Uncle Jonathan, Uncle Jonathan," he kept yelling, obviously delighted to see me. I wrapped him in my arms, and hugged him tightly.

"Who's that?" He asked pointing at Mac.

"He's your new Uncle Mac. His real name is Cornelius, but you don't want to be spreading that around." Junior laughed.

I put him down just as Sammy ran up to me and wrapped his arms around my leg. Sammy is three. He just hugged my leg without saying a word. I had to pull him off me so I could walk into the house.

Jenna was running toward me. She's two years younger than I, but she was always the feisty one. "You bastard," she yelled at me as she stuck her face in mine. "How could you not tell me that you were gay, and about your partner? I could kill you for not confiding in me." Then she put her arms around my neck and started to cry.

Allen walked up behind her and stroked her back. He looked at Mac, stuck out his hand and said, "Hi Mac, I'm Allen, and I want to be the first to welcome you to the family."

The children had been pre-fed. Jenna put Sammy to bed right after we arrived, and permitted Junior to watch television for a while longer in the den.

When we sat down to dinner, the first course was grapefruit halves. "Start talking, buster," Jenna said to me, and I did. I began my narrative going back to when I was barely reaching puberty. I admitted to my sister that I knew I was gay even then, and how I tried to hide it by doing all the wrong things.

By the time we reached dessert, they knew how unhappy I was with Marsha, but none of it was Marsha's fault. I told them how I met Mac and how we used to see each other every time I got to Buffalo; how I had been robbed and how Mac was the detective on the case; how I met Jonathan Mallory and afterwards his partner, Jake. I told them about the biggest shock of all; finding out that my best friend in Buffalo was gay, and how I met his partner, Dominick.

My story progressed to buying the apartment and how the real estate agent turned out to be Izzy's daughter, who had a gay son.

I laughed when I told her that Izzy asked me to ask Tom to mentor his grandson, and that apparently I was the only one who didn't know that my friend was gay. When the narrative was concluded, Jenna asked, how after all these years of silence, I got the courage to tell Marsha. This was the only lie I told them. I described the hickey, but I attributed it to Mac not to Jake.

"When she saw it, she thought it was another woman, so I took the opportunity to tell her that it was a man. She didn't believe me until I showed her Mac's picture. She kicked me right out of the house."

When dinner was over, I volunteered to put Junior to bed. He was half asleep already and I met little resistance. The others cleared the table, loaded the dishwasher and we went into the den.

"Does anyone want an after dinner drink?" Allen asked. Mac took him up on the offer, but I declined. I was the designated driver.

Jenna kept staring at Mac, and I knew she was dying to say something. "Mac," she finally spoke up. "Without taking anything away from my handsome husband and my equally handsome brother, I gotta tell you, that you are drop dead gorgeous. Forgive me if I drool. I always said that the best looking guys, in fact all the good guys, were gay."

"Why thank you, Jenna. That was so sweet of you. As soon as we square away our condo, we'll make a family dinner. You have two great kids."

"You two would make great parents," Allen said. "You should consider adoption, or better yet, a surrogate mother."

"Wow, that's a heavy thought," Mac said. "Who knows what the future might bring?"

Chapter Thirteen

The next morning I drove myself to the train station. We didn't want to risk that nobody would be home when the movers arrived. At the office, I kept calling Mac every five minutes to find out if the truck was there yet. Finally, he told me to calm down and he would call me when it got there. At 10:30 AM he called to say that the movers had just brought the first load up the service elevator. I breathed a sigh of relief.

Most of us in the office, including Izzy, ordered lunch from a local deli. The only time I went out for lunch was when I had a date with Allen or had some other errand to run. This day I was eating in. When the food arrived, I was too excited to eat, and Izzy's eagle eye spotted my anxiety.

"What's wrong with you, *boychick*?" he asked me.

"Our furniture is being delivered as we speak. I won't have to sleep on an air mattress tonight."

"Well, sonny, you're next to useless here. Why don't you go home and help Mac get things organized?"

"Thanks, boss," I said. "I really appreciate that."

"Sure, sure," Izzy said. "I'll take it out of your hide another time."

Unfortunately I had to wait an hour and a half for the next train to Valley Stream and beyond. The non rush hour schedule was sparse. When I arrived, I could see the moving truck at the building entrance. I peeked in and was pleased to see that it was empty. When I got to the apartment, Mac was just handing his check to the mover. He introduced me to the mover, Zack, and his son, Sandy.

"Well, thank you Mr. MacNeal," Zack said. We want to get going so we can be back home by midnight."

As soon as they left, Mac hugged me and we set to work. Our bedroom furniture was all in place. Mac had marked every package with what the contents were, and what room to place it in. There were several boxes in the bedroom, and we found one marked 'bed sheets.'

"Let's make the bed. That way it will be ready for us. We might be too tired later tonight," Mac suggested. He was right. We never went to bed that night until all the boxes in the bedroom were opened and the contents put away. We also emptied our suitcases and put all our socks, shirts and underwear away in drawers. We broke the boxes down and placed them near the dumpster. Every owner has a storage bin. I ran to a nearby hardware store and bought a lock. When I returned, we put our suitcases in the storage bin and secured the bin with the new lock.

Then we attacked the boxes in the kitchen. There were seven of them. It took us four hours to empty the boxes and put away the myriad of stuff that makes up a well stocked kitchen. We agreed that we had done well, and that was it for the night. We also realized that we had not eaten dinner, and we were too pooped to prepare something.

There was an all night diner very close to the apartment. We went there, and we each had a hamburger on a bun with French fries. I could feel my arteries filling with cholesterol, but at the moment I didn't care. To add insult to injury, I ended the meal with a chocolate milk shake. Mac had a cup of coffee, but I let him have a sip of my shake. We lingered for awhile before returning home.

"Could we go shopping for a guest bedroom set first thing in the morning?" I asked. "Tom and Dominick will be here before we know it. We only have eleven more cartons to unpack in the living room and dining room, and three in the bathroom. I'm sure we'll be finished before the weekend is over."

"Yes," Mac agreed. "Let's make tomorrow a shopping day. I'd also like to buy some outdoor furniture for our terrace."

"Let's go home now and celebrate our first night in our own home in a real bed," I suggested. Or maybe I pleaded.

We rushed home and into the shower. Mac kept soaping my ass and his cock. He wanted desperately to fuck me, but I wouldn't let him. I wanted to make love in our bed. When I realized that he was going to rape me, if I didn't let him enter me, I shut the water and got out of the shower. I dried Mac's magnificent body and he dried mine. He was just too hot for any more preliminaries. He lubed his cock and my ass and threw me on my back. He lifted my legs and to my delight, he entered me. and not very slowly. He met minimal resistance.

He pumped slowly, easily, not wishing to cum too soon, but it was no use. He came in a few short strokes. I had seen this happen before and I knew he would be able to go again. He never lost his erection, and after the sensitivity passed, he fucked me hard and properly. His cock was massaging my prostate, and he did indeed cum again, just after I did.

We cleansed ourselves, and after a few short minutes, we both fell into an exhausted sleep. We usually wake up about six in the morning so we were shocked to find that it was 8 AM when we awakened on Saturday morning.

The kitchen was all set for living, and we made a breakfast of bacon and eggs, toast and coffee. After we cleaned the kitchen and put the dirty dishes in the dishwasher, we scoured the fry pan. We then got dressed and went to shop for furniture. I can't tell you how excited that made me, and Mac seemed equally excited. In fact, he said to me, "This is the first time I have ever gone shopping for furniture, or any other domestic stuff, with a partner. I love it."

We went to one of those big chain furniture stores that promised delivery within 24 hours. We bought an attractive, modern, five piece bedroom set for the guest room. We did not get top of the line, figuring that this furniture would not be used too often. Then we bought an outdoor patio set that cost more than the bedroom set. The store promised delivery on Monday morning. By agreement, I was to pay for the bedroom set and we were to share the cost of the patio furniture.

From there we went to Macy's and bought linen for the new bed which was queen size. Our bed is king size and that's the only size linen Mac brought from Buffalo. We returned home in time for lunch. While I started to make some deli sandwiches, Mac unpacked the boxes in the bath room. He had packed his towels, wash cloths, paper towels, and toilet paper, as well as his remaining toiletries. Everything was put away by the time I had the sandwiches ready. He broke down the boxes to take to the dumpster later.

"Beer or soda?" I asked Mac

"I think I'd like a coke," he said.

We ate rather quickly, and began to tackle the living room, which had fewer boxes than the dining room. Knick knacks quickly filled the end tables and the coffee table, and four more boxes were broken down. Mac started working on the dining room boxes while I made two trips to the dumpster with the flattened boxes. I didn't realize it, but by this time it was almost 4 PM. After getting rid of the last of the flattened boxes, I headed for the elevator and there stood Jake. I forgot he was off for the remainder of the weekend.

"I hope you don't mind," he said, "but I was lonely. Also I thought I could help you unpack."

"Maybe you can," I said. "Believe it or not, we are on our last room, the dining room is almost done."

When we got upstairs, we found that Mac had unpacked three more boxes and piled the contents on the dining room table. "Let's put these in the breakfront before we open more," I said. While we were doing that, Jake took the flattened boxes and the wrapping paper to the dumpster. When he returned, Mac and I had almost put away all the contents of the boxes, which included an expensive china set, service for twelve, that Mac's mother had given him.

The three of us emptied the remaining boxes, again piling the contents on the dining room table. There was a set of sterling silver that Mac had inherited from an aunt, and an assortment of serving pieces. There were platters, butter dishes, salad tongs, salt and pepper shakers, napkin holders, and other dining room accessories. I wondered at how Mac had accumulated all these assets. While he and I found a place for all these things, Jake again broke down the boxes and took them and the wrapping paper to the dumpster. It required several trips.

All that remained to open, and we agreed to hold them until tomorrow, were pictures and mirrors in special boxes. In all, there were seven of them still sitting in the front entrance hall.

"I came to take you out to dinner," Jake said. "I didn't think you would have time to prepare something for yourselves. I know a great gay bar and restaurant in the Village. You guys need to relax for a bit. I'm driving so you can drink to your heart's content. Best of all, it's my treat and no arguing."

"We need to shower," I told Jake. "How about you?"

"If I can borrow a fresh pair of briefs," he said.

"You'll have to settle for boxers," Mac said.

Our shower had plenty of room for two, but three was a little cramped. That was fine with all of us. We fondled and let our fingers enter forbidden holes. We stroked our erections, but could not bend down to taste. I think I heard Jake say, "I'm sleeping over tonight." I was too lost in pleasure to be sure, but I knew that Mac and I wanted him to.

Reluctantly we turned off the water and stepped out of the shower. We dressed, and headed for Jake's car which was parked in the street. "Until Mac gets his car, you can use space number sixteen when you come over," I told him.

Street parking spaces were hard to come by in Greenwich Village, especially on a Saturday night. Parking garages were just as rare and filled up quickly. It was relatively early when we got there, and we lucked out. Jake was able to secure a metered space. We pulled out all our change and were able to fill the meter to maximum.

Jake had called ahead and made reservations. Even with reservations we had a fifteen minute wait. We went to the bar, where Jake was carded, even though all he ordered was a coke. I had a gin and tonic, and Mac had a scotch and soda. The three of us enjoyed the eye candy, both behind the bar and on the bar stools. It did not escape my attention that there were plenty of guys who considered us to be eye candy as well.

The dinner menu was very gourmet, but Jake insisted we order anything on it. Mac and I ordered filet mignon and Jake followed suit. Since it was Saturday night, the restaurant provided a floor show. We were treated to an assortment of drag acts. Some were great and some should never have been allowed on the floor. Nevertheless, we enjoyed the show and after dinner we lingered at our table, enjoying the show and our company.

Eventually, I could see that Jake was getting antsy. It wasn't hard to see that he was very horny. I had not been with him for several days now. "You look like you're ready to go home now." I said to him, giving him an opening. I had reached a point in my life where once a day or every other day was satisfactory enough, but I must be honest and admit that when one of my boys was added to the mix, I got extra horny. I know for sure that Mac did also. In short, I was ready to go home and play also.

When we got home, Jake parked indoors at number sixteen. I now knew which parking spaces were Robert's and Bob's, and both their cars were parked. It was not yet 10 o'clock when we got into the apartment. I called them immediately, and told them that we had a guest that I would like them to meet, and I invited them to breakfast. They accepted. We had pushed ourselves hard in the unpacking process and we were ready for company. We agreed that we would hang the pictures and mirrors after breakfast.

But for now we had other things on our minds. We undressed hastily and climbed into bed with Jake in the middle. This night, both Mac and I applied Mac's famous trip around the world to our boy, Jake. He sighed, whined, moaned and groaned, and came twice before either of us even took his cock into our mouths. I marveled at the prowess of youth, but I didn't envy Jake. I had paid my dues, and I wouldn't want to repeat any part of my life. It was perfect right now, even if I did cum slightly fewer times a week. After Jake had a third orgasm, this time spilling his juices down my throat, he lay spent and totally exhausted.

"Please fuck me," Mac said to me. "You owe me for last night." I happily obliged, while Jake watched us. Of course, he got hard again, and he started to stroke his cock. Mac came first, cumming all over his chest. Immediately after that, I happily filled his ass to capacity, and damned if Jake didn't stroke himself to a fourth orgasm. I hoped that I would be able to wake him when Bob and Robert came for breakfast the next morning.

We all fell into a deep and peaceful sleep. It was the kind of sleep that comes when you are happy and satisfied. Mac and I woke up about 6:30 and showered together. We agreed to let Jake sleep, while we set the table, put up the coffee, and took the rolls and bagels out of the freezer.

We both put on a pair of jeans and a tee shirt (no underwear). We wore only slippers on our feet. We set the kitchen table for five, and took out the butter and margarine. We put the rolls and bagels in a breadbasket and provided a sharp knife to cut them. This was the first time Mac and I were entertaining as a couple, and I was really excited.

When everything was done, Mac grabbed Jake's legs and dragged him out of bed. He literally carried him to the shower, and told him that it was time to rise and shine. Mac turned on the water and pushed Jake inside. "This is cruel and unusual punishment," Jake whined. When we were sure that he was operating on his own steam, we left him alone in the bathroom.

Jake was out of the shower and drying himself when Bob and Robert arrived. They looked around and Bob said, Except for the pictures in the front hall, you guys look like you have been here forever."

"We're getting the guest bedroom suite and patio furniture tomorrow morning. In the meantime we hope to put up the wall hangings after breakfast," Mac told them.

Bob piped in. "Please let Robert help you. He's the official picture hanger among all our friends. The nerd uses geometry, and everything comes out picture perfect, if you'll excuse the pun."

"You're on," Mac and I yelled out in unison.

"So where's your guest?" Bob asked. We had folded up the air mattress and we had placed it in the trunk of Jake's car the evening before. He would be coming out of the master bedroom, when he was finally ready. I wondered if they would realize that he had slept with us. Well if they did they would only be jealous when they saw him.

"He just got out of the shower," I said. "He should be ready any second and then we'll eat."

About two minutes later out came Jake. As logy as he had been moments ago, he was now a bundle of energy. Again I thought, *let's hear it for youth.* When he came out of the bedroom, I saw two jaws drop. I made the introductions and told everyone to sit at the kitchen table.

"Mac and I have adopted Jake and his partner, Jonathan. We think of them as our sons," I explained.

"Are there any more like you at home? I'm all for adoption," Robert joked.

"Sorry Robert, I'm an only child," Jake quipped back.

"We are really so happy you guys bought here," Bob said. "There are two other gay couples in the building. They're nice people, but both couples are retired and in their late seventies. They hang together a lot, but you guys are closer in age to us, and we would sure like to be friends."

"I don't see why not," Mac said. I was beginning to learn that Mac was a lot more outgoing than I.

"We have friends from Buffalo who are moving down right after this semester ends," I informed them. My intent was to make them realize that we could not give them all of our leisure time. Mac realized what I was doing and gave me a funny look. "They are coming down during spring break to look for a house. They'll be staying with us," I added, "so you'll get to meet them."

"That's wonderful," Robert said.

"I can't wait to meet them, and we have some great friends that we'd like you to meet," Bob echoed. I think he was getting back at me.

After the breakfast mess was cleaned up, Mac and Robert set about hanging the pictures and mirrors, while Jake and I broke down the boxes, removed the heavy wrappings, and took everything to the dumpster. By now I was feeling sorry for the sanitation department. At least we had flattened all the boxes.

Mac told Robert where everything had hung before, but Robert suggested several changes, which Mac seemed to approve of. Robert measured everything three times before a single nail was put in the wall. It took a couple of hours, but when everything was hung, our apartment looked warm, welcoming and homey. I particularly liked the mirror in the front hall which hung over a small table. I knew that the table would house our keys when we came home at night.

When all that was done, the five of us sat and chatted for a while, and got to know each other better. At about noon, Bob and Robert excused themselves, saying that they were visiting friends that afternoon. We were done with handshakes. Everyone kissed them when they left.

Shortly after they left, Jake said that he wanted to leave Mac and me to enjoy our new home and have a lazy Sunday afternoon, and he left too.

"Let's do something domestic and Sunday like," I said, so we went to a movie matinee. When we came home after the movie we started to prepare an early dinner. We had skipped lunch because breakfast had been more like brunch.

After dinner, we sat with our feet up on the coffee table watching TV. Then as we were getting ready for bed, Mac grabbed me in a bear hug.

"Was today domestic enough for you?" he asked

"God yes," I replied. "Promise me every Sunday will be like this."

"Next Sunday we'll invite Allen, Jenna and the boys for lunch." How much more domestic can we get?"

On Monday morning, Mac waited for the new furniture to be delivered, and by 11 AM the bedroom and the terrace were all set up. Wrappings and boxes were disposed of. Mac looked around the apartment and was more than pleased. The empty rooms had become a home for him and for me. Mac felt good all over, but he knew that he couldn't sit around the apartment for four more days without me. He'd go crazy.

He called the precinct and spoke to a Miss Murphy in Human Resources, begging her to let him start the next day instead of the following Monday.

"Are you kidding?" she asked. "You could have come in yesterday. There were two positions available when we interviewed you, and we haven't filled the other one yet. Crime never stops! Please report to my office tomorrow morning at 8 AM. The administrative paperwork alone will take a half a day."

"How about if I come in this afternoon and get all the paper work out of the way, so I can really start tomorrow?"

"Perfect," Miss Murphy cooed. "Be here at 1 PM."

"See ya," Mac said, and hung up. He called to let me know what was going on and I wished him well. He made himself a salad for lunch, and then he checked our crisp new phone books. He called a nearby cab company to take him to his new precinct. As he waited for the cab in the lobby of our building, his heart was beating like a drum. Later he told me, "I felt like I was going to my first day of school."

Chapter Fourteen

When I got home that night and parked my car, I saw a Ford Crown Victoria in space sixteen. It had no distinguishing markings, and for all intents and purposes it was a civilian car. Of course, I knew that it was Detective MacNeal's chariot.

I rushed to the elevator and when it didn't come soon enough for me, I bounded up the four flights of stairs. I threw open our front door, and immediately I could smell the aroma of hearty tomato sauce. Mac was in the kitchen preparing our dinner of linguini and meat balls. Another delicious aroma was coming from the oven where Mac was baking garlic bread.

"I conned Gino into giving me his recipe for garlic bread," Mac informed me as he kissed me. "I gave him my blood oath to tell nobody else, so don't even ask me."

I hung up my coat laughing all the way to the front hall closet. When I got back to the kitchen I asked what I could do, and Mac said, "Well it's nice to eat pasta off a plate. You might set the table for us. Make it the dining room table. Let's do fine dining tonight. Take out two wine glasses while you are at it. I busied myself setting the table while Mac turned off the oven and took out the garlic bread, which he placed in a bread basket. He placed the basket in the middle of the dining room table, and took a bottle of red wine from the kitchen counter. He must have bought it on the way home. He poured the wine into the two wine glasses, and bade me follow him onto the terrace.

It was a late winter evening, and still a bit chilly, but for a guy fresh from Buffalo, it felt like a Miami Beach evening. We sat on our new patio chairs and Mac toasted us as we sipped the wine. I went and got a sweater, and still I was shivering. Mac was sitting there with only a tee shirt on, and he was fine with the forty degree temperature. *Give it a year,* I thought, *and he won't be so macho about the temperature out here.*

He told me about his tedious day of filling out documents, taking a physical exam, being assigned an auto, and meeting his new partner.

"Tell me about him." I said.

"Him's a her," Mac said.

That made me feel a lot better. By God, I realized I was jealous and laughed inwardly. "Tell me about her. Is she straight or lesbian?"

"I was trying to figure it out myself." Mac commented. "I imagine after a few days working together, I'll find out. I intend to tell her I'm gay right up front."

"Do you think I'll ever be as brave as you are when it comes to telling people that I'm gay?"

"I don't know," Mac answered. "Let's see how it all plays out. I'm satisfied for now that when we are alone together, you aren't shy about showing me just how gay you are." He reached across the patio table and squeezed my hand.

"God, your hand is cold," he said.

"Yes," I said. You can stay out here if you want to. I'm going inside where it's nice and warm."

"OK," Mac answered. "The pasta should be ready by now."

We had just seated ourselves at the dining room table to begin our meal, when my cell phone rang. Few people had our land line number yet.

"MacNeal/Walters residence," I said jokingly.

"Gallini/Baker residence here," I heard Tom's voice mocking me.

"Hey man, we're just sitting down to dinner. Can I call you back in about half an hour?"

"It's OK, buddy. This will only take a second. Dom and I have ants in our pants, and we decided to come down next weekend. Actually, we're arriving Thursday evening and staying until Sunday night. Is that OK and is your invitation still open?"

"Absolutely! That's fantastic. What great news."

"Can you set us up with your real estate agent?'

"Yes. In fact, I'll ask her to pick you up on Friday morning because we'll both be at work. Mac started his new job early, so now we can eat this week."

"Very funny," Tom jeered. "I'll E Mail you the flight information. If you can't pick us up let me know, and we'll take a cab. Don't tell Izzy we're coming. He'll want to take up precious time. We'll see him at spring break. Also don't tell Jake, but Jonathan is coming with us as a surprise for Jake. He's also booked on our spring break flight. Now go back to your dinner. Ciao."

"I heard it all," Mac said. "How great is that? I can't wait for the weekend. We'll drop Jonathan off at Jake's apartment first. He'll be so happily surprised."

After dinner I called Marlene at home and Billy answered. "Hey guy," I said. "We haven't forgotten you. As soon as my friends from Buffalo move down here we are going to ask your mother if you can spend a day with us. We'll also include our teen age friends, so start writing down all your questions."

"That's so cool," Billy said. "Hold on and I'll get my mom."

Marlene greeted me warmly. I told her that Tom and Dom were coming in this Thursday evening, and wanted to see as many houses as possible. I told her that it would be extra special nice if she showed them houses in our neighborhood. I asked her not to tell her dad about Tom being here, because he wanted to use the brief time he and Dominick had for house hunting. Besides, they would see plenty of him when they came down for spring break in a few short weeks.

"They won't have a car," I said. "Can you pick them up Friday morning and that way you can get to see our place furnished and in use?"

"Sounds great. I'm really anxious to see what you have done. While I've got you, I just heard that your closing is set for two weeks from tomorrow morning so you guys will have to arrange to take the morning off. I'll give you all the details when I see you this weekend."

"That's such exciting news," I said to Mac while we were cleaning up the dinner mess. "What can we eat to celebrate."

"Listen baby," Mac said. When I first met you, you were as hard as a rock. I don't mind some little amount of love handles, but you are beginning to put on the pounds. You and I are going to begin using the exercise room in the basement, and I want you to promise to stop showing your happiness with food. I appreciate how happy you are, and I even take all the credit, but it's time to get real. Is it a deal?"

"Deal!" I said.

On Monday evening after work, Mac informed me that his partner, Diana Durning, was no lesbian. "Her boyfriend picked her up after work to take her home because her car was being serviced." Mac smacked his lips and said, "Her boyfriend, Roy, is some hunk. I wouldn't throw him out of bed."

"Should I be jealous?" I asked.

"No way. On the Kinsey scale he's a ten for heterosexuality. Diana told him I was gay, and he was actually glad about it. I can understand why. Diana is very attractive."

"Have they assigned you any interesting cases?" I asked.

"Yes, but it's tough to talk about. A boy in Billy's school was ambushed by several other boys wearing ski masks. They beat him up, but he'll be all right. It was classified as a hate crime because they kept calling him faggot. I'm going to call Billy after dinner tonight. I want to know if he knows the boy. If he does maybe he can give me some information without getting involved. I want to get those bastards. Even Diana said that hate crimes make her madder than any other crime, even domestic violence. I like that lady, and she wants to meet you. We'll have to double date one day."

Even though it was Mac who had the interesting job, and he was full of stories each evening, he always made sure to ask me about new products I was marketing. He would even get excited at the prospect of using some new gadget or tasting some new cereal. I didn't care if he was pretending interest in my job, I was grateful that he never failed to include me in our nightly discussions. Maybe he knew a secret I had learned. Sex was ten times better when you and your partner communicated, not only about your sexual needs, but your daily lives also.

At last it was Thursday. We ate our dinner, watched the early evening news and finally it was time to drive to the airport. We used Mac's car so that our personal car would get less use. Besides, the Crown Victoria was bigger than my car. We had previously told Jake that Tom and Dominick were arriving this evening, and he wanted to come along to the airport. We lied and told him that we were going to Izzy's after we picked them up, and he would meet them the next day. Jonathan wanted to surprise him by walking in on him at their apartment.

The plane was late of course, over an hour and a half, due to bad weather in Buffalo. So what else is new? We went to a coffee shop and Mac ordered coffee and a Danish pastry. Remembering his words to me, I ordered coffee only, black, and no sugar. Mac smiled at me and gave me a thumbs up. We had used the condo exercise room twice since our talk, and I was watching my food intake. So far I had lost three pounds in two days. My goal was fifteen.

Finally they arrived. The flight was shorter than the wait. Hugs and kisses all around. All they had with them were carry-on bags, and we didn't have to go to baggage claim. Hallelujah!

We threw the bags in the trunk and the three travelers sat in the rear. "First stop is Jake's place in Oceanside," I announced. "We're only going to drop Jonathan off," I told Tom and Dom. You'll meet Jake tomorrow. Marlene is picking you guys up at 10 AM tomorrow. She has a number of places for you to look at tomorrow and Saturday. She figured she'll give you a break on Sunday. If you don't find anything, you'll continue the search during spring break."

When we got to Jake's apartment, Mac popped the trunk. Jonathan got out, grabbed his bag and closed the trunk. I swear I could see that his pants were tenting. He bounded towards the front door. Once we saw that he was safely in the building, we headed for home.

Tom and Dom loved our apartment, especially the vista from the terrace. "If you change your minds about living in a condo, there are at least two apartments for sale in this building. I understand one of them is a three bedroom unit and is larger than this one. The other is exactly the same as this one. There's a gay couple lives right above us. They have the same apartment, but you would never know it, because it is decorated and furnished so differently. They want to meet you. We are all having dinner together tomorrow evening, Jake and Jonathan included."

Even though I was dieting, Mac put up coffee and took a cake out of the fridge. He had bought it at a local bakery, and it was iced with the words, *Welcome Home.* I vowed not to touch it, but Mac urged me to have a sliver. While we were preparing this decadent feast, Tom and Dom were using the guest bath room shower to freshen up. It was the first time it had been used.

When they were finished and dry, they came out of the guest room wearing only bed room slippers and both of them were very hard. Obviously they had played in the shower.

"I wouldn't want you to feel self conscious or anything," I said and I started to strip as well.

"What the hell," Mac uttered and he began to strip too.

We were enjoying our coffee and cake when Tom said. "I want to tell you guys that after Mac left Buffalo, Jonathan started to come around to visit with us, and we began to have sex together. He told me that you guys and Jake were doing as much, so I guess it's all right. We just wanted to be honest and let you know."

"It's more important that they tell each other and I'm sure they did," Mac said. "Equally as important is who is sleeping with whom tonight?" That having been said, he broke out laughing, stood up, and enveloped Dominick in a bear hug as he grabbed Dom's erect cock. "I figure that Wallie and Tom want to continue to make up for all those years they wanted each other and never acted on their cravings."

Tom stood up and kissed Mac on the cheek. "Thanks," he said to Mac. "You are a man of great perception."

The four of us pitched in to clean up the kitchen and load the dishwasher. Mac and Dom went into our bedroom because they were both such big men, and the bed in the master bedroom was larger than the one in the guest room. The rooms were across the hall from one another and the doors remained open. For the next two hours, I could hear the sounds of love making coming from across the hall. It made me extra hot, and I know it did as much for Tom. The noises worked in two directions, and I am sure the moans Tom and I were making, were turning on Mac and Dom as well. In fact, my cock was buried deep in Tom's mouth when I heard Mac's familiar screech, and I knew that he had just cum. I had been holding back my orgasm, but when I heard him, that did it for me, and I let loose, screaming louder than Mac. Eventually we all fell asleep, contentedly wrapped up in each other's arms. As I fell asleep, I remember thinking, "Love is such a wonderful thing."

I was awakened by the shrill sound of the alarm clock coming from across the hall. As I crossed the hall to use my own shower, Dom passed me on the way back to the guest room. "You guys can sleep late, but remember Marlene will be here at 10," I reminded him.

Mac and I wanted to make as little noise as possible so we left the keys on the hall table, and slipped out of the house. We had breakfast at the coffee shop down at the corner of our street before heading to work. We had invited my sister and her family, Jake and Jonathan, and Bob and Robert to dinner that evening instead of for Sunday lunch, because we wanted them to meet Tom and Dom and Jake and Jonathan. We would have invited Izzy, Gloria, Marlene and Billy also, but Tom didn't want Izzy to know that he was in town. We decided to invite the others next week.

It was a pretty big crowd for us to attempt to cook for, so we assigned McLean's Deli the task of doing the catering. Jake was thrilled to do it. In fact, he called me twice that day at work to let me know what he decided to add to the menu, if it was all right with me. I had to remind him that I had left it all to him. "Jonathan and I will try to get there early and set everything up," he said. He had our key, of course, and we had his.

Fortunately I had an exceptionally busy day at work, and the time went fast. The ever compassionate Izzy even said to me once, "It'll be nice when Tom gets here to help you with so much work."

"You bet," I agreed.

I pulled into my parking space and noted that Mac wasn't home yet. Neither were Bob and Robert. I hoped that Jake and Jonathan were there already, and setting up. When I opened up the door the aroma that wafted into my nostrils almost sent me reeling. Jake was using the dining room table as a buffet. Before I had a chance to see what he was putting on it, Jonathan jumped on me and devoured me with kisses.

"Hey, hey, sonny," I joked. "Didn't Jake satisfy you last night?"

"You know damn well he did, pops," Jonathan joked back.

I went over to examine the table. The first chafing dish contained stuffed cabbage. The next contained chicken parmesan. After that there were several cold platters with mixed deli meats; turkey, roast beef, and ham. There were breadbaskets full of rye breads and dinner rolls. There were platters of veggies with dips, and finally plenty of condiments were on the table. Jake had even supplied all the flatware and napkins. He had spread the dining room chairs out in the living room and there were folding trays opened up and within easy reach of each chair.

"Dessert is in the fridge," Jake told me, as if I even noticed that there was no dessert on the table.

"Everything looks absolutely delicious and the presentation is superb," I complimented Jake. Then I gave him a big kiss on the lips. Jonathan joined us and we stood, holding each other tightly in a communal hug. Finally I said, I'm going to wash up and change my clothes. "I'm too dressed up for an informal party."

The first guests to arrive were Jenna, Allen and the boys. They handed me an envelope and said that it was a gift for our new house. When I introduced Jake and Jonathan to them, I explained that they were our adopted sons, and in her usual flippant manner Jenna said, "I'm glad you told me that they are adopted. You aren't good looking enough to have spawned two such gorgeous young men."

We set Allen Jr. and Sammy down in front of the TV in our bedroom, and I suggested to Jenna that she might want to feed them first. "They're quiet now," she said, "so let's wait until they start acting up. In the meantime give us the two cent tour of the apartment."

Tom and Dominick were the next to arrive. Marlene had dropped them off in front of the condo. They looked tired but happy when they arrived. I introduced them to Allen and Jenna. Jenna said to Tom, "It's a real pleasure to meet you Tom. Wallie has spoken of you so often over the years." Then they went into their bedroom to wash and freshen up.

Mac, Bob and Robert were still not here. Mac's job was not nine to five, and he could not always get away whenever he wanted to, but Robert and Bob should have been home hours ago. I rang their apartment and got the answering machine. The old feeling of dread poured onto me like a tsunami, and I suddenly could not breathe. I calmed myself and called Mac. His cell phone went to voice mail. Now I was scared. I left the others and went into the bedroom where the boys were watching a cartoon channel. "Do you mind if I put on the news for just a second," I asked the boys.

They didn't answer me so I just switched channels. Every network channel was showing the same thing. Some student had gone into Valley Stream High School shooting a high powered rifle. Six students and one teacher were confirmed dead, and several other students and teachers were wounded. In order to get to the dead and wounded, the police had been forced to take out the student terrorist, but not before he wounded two police officers. One of them was not expected to survive. I was now filled with more than just dread. Billy was a student at Valley Stream High, and Robert taught there. Mac would have answered the call to get to the high school along with the other policemen. I felt that my happiness was about to be taken away from me, and I would be miserable until my life ended.

Bob taught in a high school in the next town. Surely he would have heard the news, and rushed over to Valley Stream. I kicked myself for not having gotten his cell phone number. I went into the living room and in a sobbing voice I told the others what was going on, and why I was so worried. I finished talking and everyone was silent. I think each person there was praying in his own way.

My land line rang and I had the ring set so loudly, I nearly hit the ceiling. "Hello," I screamed into the phone.

"Wallie, my boy, It's Izzy. Is Mac home? Can he find out the names of the students who were killed? Marlene and I came down to the high school, but the cops won't let us near the place. Maybe Mac can find out something. We're going crazy."

"Izzy," I sobbed. "I can't reach Mac. He's not answering his cell phone. I'm going crazy too."

Chapter Fifteen

There was nothing any of us could do, so we sat and waited and watched television. We saw vivid images of body bags being taken from the building and we all wept. Jenna ran into the bedroom where the kids were watching cartoons on TV and she hugged them. At last, the students remaining in the building were taken out about a dozen at a time. They were escorted beyond the police barriers and greeted by grateful, but very hysterical parents. I searched the faces of the students, but the cameras were too far away to make a positive identification.

I tried to find Mac among the policemen, but they were all in uniform. Mac was a plain clothes detective. He would be just another figure in the crowd. I suggested to Jenna that she might want to take the kids home, but she didn't want to leave me. Allen told her to take the kids and go home because all of this activity would certainly frighten them. He said that he would stay with me. He would sleep on the sofa if he had to. Jake, Jonathan, Tom and Dominick insisted that the whole family should go home, and they would stay. They promised to call immediately with any news. After much pleading, Allen took his family home. He gave Jake his cell phone number in case they heard something while they were still en route. In turn, Jake gave them plenty of food in aluminum containers.

At some point one of the TV reporters announced that a sweep of the school turned up no more bodies. The carnage had all taken place in the gym during a phys-ed class. The murdered teacher was the gym teacher. All the victims, including the shooter, had been removed and taken to the morgue for identification. The wounded had been taken to three nearby hospitals. All the while I kept dialing Mac's number, but he wasn't answering.

The scene on the TV shifted to the hospital where the wounded policeman had been taken. A doctor was reporting on his condition. His wounds were critical but he was expected to survive. It wasn't Mac, but the dead policeman remained unidentified pending notification of next of kin. Mac had put my name down to call in case of emergency. So far no calls had been received.

When finally the phone rang at about 9 PM, I was too scared to pick it up and Tom answered it. I stopped breathing until I heard Tom say, "Mac, it's you. Thank God."

I grabbed the phone from Tom and sobbed into the handset. "Mac, are you hurt?"

"No, I'm fine. Listen to me, please. I'm sorry I couldn't call sooner, but we were pretty busy here. Billy is fine. He was at the other end of the building when all this came down. His teacher locked as many of the class as he could in a big storage closet, and the rest in a broom closet. Billy was one of the last out of the building. When I spotted him, I grabbed him and hustled him to Marlene. She and Izzy were nearly hysterical, but still Marlene introduced me to Izzy. You know what the old codger said to me, between sobs, that is. 'I should have known that Wallie's boyfriend would be a hero.' He hugged me and kissed me and muttered, 'Sorry we had to meet this way.' I told them to get out of there and get Billy home.

"I also found Robert in a classroom, comforting some hysterical kids. I took them all outside to their parents, and Bob took Robert home. At the moment I don't know when I'll get home, but I'm fine so have the party without me."

"Do you know who did this and why?" I asked.

"Yes and yes," Mac answered. "It was the kid who was the victim of the hate crime I'm investigating. We've got to get into the schools and teach these kids the consequences of bullying. In spite of all the school massacres, the schools are still not cracking down on bullying. I don't know if the kid knew his attackers and targeted them, or if the shooting was random. Unless someone tells us who the attackers were, we'll never know. I gotta go now. I love you!"

We hung up, and I breathed a sigh of relief. "I guess we better eat some of this great food," I suggested.

"I'd better call Allen," Jake said.

We all took a plate of food, when my doorbell rang. It was Bob. "Sorry to spoil the party," he said. "Robert's a wreck. I got him into bed and gave him a couple of sleeping pills. He's out like a light."

"Come in and meet the guys," I said. Bob had already met Jake, who was on the phone talking to Allen. "This handsome young stud is Jake's partner, Jonathan," I said, and turning to Tom and Dominick, I introduced them next. Everybody shook hands and regretted the circumstances. "Things can only get better," I commented.

Bob had no appetite, but we forced him to eat. While all of us were eating, the mood lightened somewhat. I noticed that Bob was in an animated conversation with Dominick. The two teachers really hit it off.

"My god," I said to Tom. "In all the excitement, I forgot to ask what happened with you and Marlene."

"I was waiting for you to remember, but I didn't want to say anything while surrounded by all this tragedy. Actually. I have a bit of a story to tell. Are you all ready?" We all quieted down to listen.

"After you and Mac left for work, Dom and I got to talking. We think your apartment is spacious, beautiful and more than enough for our needs. We began to wonder why we would want to get involved with lawn maintenance, roof repairs and all that goes with owning a home. So when Marlene came in, the first thing we did was show her your apartment. She absolutely loves your decor. Sorry, Wallie, our bed wasn't made. We told her that we hadn't completely made up our minds, but we wouldn't mind looking at condos as well as houses.

"She said that there were two apartments available in this building. She could show them to us unless we didn't want to be in the same building as you and Mac. We assured her that the place most in the world I would want to be, was as close to you two as possible.

"We saw the three bedroom apartment first. It's on the sixth floor. The view from the terrace is to die for, but they are asking a lot. It's probably worth it, but we don't need anything that big. The second apartment is 4J at the opposite end of the hall from you guys. It's a mirror image of your place. It's empty and ready for occupancy."

Tom paused, so I piped in. "Well???"

"We decided to make an offer and not waste time seeing houses. To make a long story short, the owners have moved to LA, and it was actually too early to call them. Marlene went back to her office and said she would call us after she spoke to them." Tom came over to me and hugged me. "They accepted our offer, and they are willing to close on June 1st, the day after our closing in Buffalo. We'll move the furniture out a day or two before the Buffalo closing so the truck can get here on June 1st. I want the name of Mac's mover," he said.

Bob was the first one to jump up and hug Dominick. Then he hugged Tom. "This is so cool," he said. I can't wait until you guys are all moved in." Then Jake, Jonathan and I hugged everybody else. Bob was not excluded.

"You haven't heard the best part," Tom said. "The reason we weren't around when you came home from work, Wallie, is that we were being interviewed by Tony and Joyce. What a farce. The whole event consisted of Dominick and Tony conversing in Italian, and Joyce flirting with me. They loved us. Tony is so hot for Dom, I'll bet we could convert him."

"How about Joyce converting you," Dom laughed.

"No way, Jose," Tom responded.

Suddenly, I felt very tired, and Jake and Jonathan must have sensed that it was time to end the evening. Jake started to put the leftovers into aluminum containers and unfortunately there were plenty of leftovers. They put the first five containers in a plastic bag and insisted that Bob take it home. Bob objected, but Jake explained that I didn't have enough room in the freezer and he would be doing us a favor.

Then he started to load my refrigerator and freezer with containers. When he absolutely could not put another container in the freezer, he put all the remaining ones in a big plastic garbage bag. "I'll put what I can in my fridge and freezer," Jake said. "I'll have to throw out the rest."

He rinsed out the chafing dishes, and Jake and Jonathan put all the catering supplies back in his van. When everything was done, they kissed us goodbye and said that they would see us tomorrow evening.

For the next hour, Tom, Dom and I cleaned up the apartment and when the dishwasher was loaded, I got it started. When we were all done, we plopped down on the sofa and I turned on the TV to get the latest on the incident. Camera crews were still at the scene. One of the reporters thrust his mike at one of the police officials, and asked, "Is there anything you can tell us about the shooter, Detective?"

The detective took the Mike and the camera panned up to his face. It was Mac. "I'll be brief," he said. "A few days ago, the boy who did the shooting, was the victim of a bullying hate crime. We can't ever be certain, but that may have been a factor in his irrational behavior. Other school massacres have also resulted directly from incidents of bullying. It's time that our schools adopted a zero tolerance for that sort of behavior. If not, this will happen again. Parents need to speak to their kids about it also. It's got to be a joint educational campaign at home and at school." While Mac was talking, a streamer crossed the bottom of the screen. 'Cornelius MacNeal, Det., Valley Stream P.D.' I couldn't help smiling when I thought how Mac was going to hate being outed as 'Cornelius.'

I found myself falling asleep on the sofa. Dominick got up, shut the TV and announced that it was time to turn in "I want to wait for Mac," I said.

"Nonsense," Tom reproached me, "he might not even come home tonight. There must be a hell of a lot of shit going on at the precinct."

"I guess you're right," I said. Tom and Dom went to the guest bedroom. I shut the apartment lights, undressed and fell asleep immediately. I must have been thoroughly exhausted or I could never have fallen asleep alone in a great big king size bed.

I was awakened by bright sunlight streaming in from the terrace and into the bedroom. Tom and Dom were on the other side of the apartment, and the light would probably not disturb them. Mac was sleeping naked on the other side of the bed. I had never heard him come in.

I got out of bed as quietly as I could, and went to the bathroom. After relieving myself, I put on a pair of boxers, and left the room. I carefully closed the door behind me. This was the first time this door had ever been closed since we moved in. The other bedroom door was wide open. I looked in and my guests were not in bed. I checked out the kitchen, and they were not there either. I looked out on the terrace and I could see them sipping coffee at the table. The outside temperature was 52 degrees, but all each had on was a pair of slacks and a tee shirt. Again I had to remember that this was like summer to these Buffalonians. Smart asses!!!!

I opened the terrace door and I said, "It looks like Mac will sleep half the day away. Let's get dressed and have breakfast out so we don't disturb him. There's a nice little coffee shop at the corner, and this will give you an opportunity to survey the neighborhood."

I dressed as quietly as I could. Mac never moved.

It was a glorious day. Spring was definitely in the air. By mid afternoon, the temperature reached the high sixties. The morning air smelled fresh, and we drank it in as we had breakfast at the corner. After breakfast we walked around the neighborhood. I pointed out the supermarket, the Cineplex and most important, the Chinese restaurant. Then to soothe Dominick, I pointed out a wonderful little Italian restaurant.

"This neighborhood is very citified compared to our neighborhood in Buffalo, or Mac's neighborhood for that matter. But I like it. It'll be great having so many amenities at hand," Tom observed.

Still not wishing to disturb Mac, we went to a small park a few streets away, and continued to enjoy the glorious morning, sitting on a park bench.

"I had hoped to celebrate the purchase of our new apartment last night in a manner we all love," Dominick said. "I hope Mac is up for it tonight. All this must be quite traumatic for him."

"I imagine it is," I commented. "He must be used to this kind of stuff, don't you think?"

"I think you're wrong," Tom said. "You can't get used to the murder of little children."

I looked at my watch. It was almost 10 o'clock. I called Marlene on her cell phone. She and Billy were at her office. "He's handling it better than I am," she told me.

"How is Izzy?" I asked.

"Pretty shook up, but he'll be all right."

"I think I'll call him," I said, but before I could dial, I got a call from Jenna. She wanted to know how Mac was doing.

"I have no idea what time he got home, but right now he's fast asleep. Tom, Dom and I went out for breakfast so as not to disturb him."

"OK," she said. "I'll check back later. Love you."

I then called Izzy. His first question was about Mac's well being. "He's fine," I said. "I have no idea what time he came home, but he's still sleeping."

"He's a regular hero, your Mac," Izzy said, "and *boychick*, he's very handsome."

The three of us returned to the apartment. Mac was still sleeping, but now he was restless. I was certain he would wake up soon. We went out on the terrace through the living room and continued to enjoy the day. From the terrace, I could peek in on Mac as well. At about 11 AM he got out of bed sporting a rather good size piss hardon. As he headed for the bathroom, I excused myself and went into the bedroom through the terrace sliding doors.

Mac was standing at the commode pissing. His cock was flaccid now. I put my arms around him and kissed him on the neck. He continued to pee. When he was done, he said, "Shower with me. I feel unclean."

Silently I stripped and went into the shower with him. I could see how exhausted he was. He was leaning against me as I soaped him thoroughly. I stroked his cock and it erected. He began to moan and I stopped.

"Would you like to cum?" I asked.

"Yes."

"How?"

"In your mouth if you don't mind. I need this badly." His voice was pleading.

"Let's go to bed," I said. It's more comfortable."

"OK."

He let me dry him. He offered no help at all. I had never seen him so exhausted. I laid him down on his back and skipped all the preliminaries. I took his cock into my mouth and began to kiss and lick it as sensuously as I could. Mac remained silent, but if I sensed he might be getting close, I withdrew and kissed him on his lips. I did this several times, but I knew at some point I could not go back. I sucked harder and harder. That's how he liked it, and he gushed into my mouth. I held him in my mouth until I had swallowed all his juice, and his limp manhood fell out. When I withdrew, I realized that he had fallen asleep again. I wet a wash cloth and cleaned him off. Then still naked, I went to find my guests.

I found them in the guest bedroom making love. "We couldn't help not seeing you and Mac from the terrace and that got us going. Join us," Tom invited me into their bed. I accepted the invitation.

When we had exhausted ourselves making love, I showered in the guest bathroom and silently got dressed again in my bedroom. The three of us prepared lunch made of last night's leftover deli. We had cokes with the sandwiches. After lunch, we returned to the terrace to enjoy the very mild temperature, and to wait for Mac to wake up. Dom and Tom actually took off their shirts and sat in their briefs.

"I'm going to love it here," Tom said.

Mac finally awoke at about 3:30, but instead of joining us, he went straight to the telephone. I didn't want to intrude so I gave him his privacy. I didn't know who he was talking to, but the conversation lasted about ten minutes, and then he came out on the terrace.

"What a glorious day," he said. "Too bad seven or eight young people are not here to enjoy it. Did you know that they finally released the names of the fatalities?" He buried his head in his hands and then he perked up.

"I just spoke to Billy. Johnny Day was the name of the shooter. He was in the same gym class as the boys who beat him up. Billy says that they constantly harassed Johnny in class, and when he appealed to the teacher, the bastard just laughed at him. All four of the boys and the teacher are among the dead, I don't know if the other victims were innocent bystanders or if they had bugged Johnny also. At any rate, this is just between us. I don't want Billy to get involved. There will be an investigation. I'll try to draw the truth out of other students who were in the gym. Not that it matters anymore, but if I can prove that the murdered boys were the perpetrators of the hate crime, it will strengthen my stand on the need to crack down on school bullies for their own sakes."

Mac became silent, and to lighten the mood, I asked Tom to give Mac the big news. When Mac was all filled in, he hugged both the men, and said that he was pleased as punch. Then my cell phone and our land phone rang simultaneously. Jenna was on my phone. I assured her that Mac was back among the living, but he was on another call and I promised he would call her back.

On the other line Mac was busy assuring Jake and Jonathan that he was really fine. "Don't forget," Jake said, "It's Saturday night and we are all going to the Village tonight for dinner and a floor show. I'll drive. My van will seat all of us comfortably. I'll pick you up about 6 PM."

When he got off the phone, Mac made a quick call to Jenna to assure her that everything was fine. He started the call by saying, "Hello Sis." I almost lost it when I heard that.

"I'll be right back," Mac said. "I want to go upstairs and check on Robert." He found our two neighbors sitting at the kitchen table sipping coffee. Robert was in his robe and badly needed a shave and a shower. Bob was dressed.

"How are you doing?" Mac asked Robert.

"I've been better, but don't worry. I intend to be all right. I need to be for the kids."

"Look," Mac said you haven't met our friends from Buffalo. They bought an apartment on the fourth floor and will be moving on June 1st. Why don't you spruce up and enjoy this weather with us on our terrace. It will do you good."

"You're right," Robert said. "I need to make a positive move. Bob you go downstairs with Mac and I'll be right along."

"I'll leave the door unlocked. Just come right in," Mac said.

We were all sipping cokes and lemonade when Robert came out on the terrace. I stood up first and introduced Robert to Dom and Tom.

"I know you, Dominick," Robert said. "Let me think a minute. What's your last name?"

"Gallini," Dom said smiling.

"Yes of course. You're Professor Gallini. You were my Spanish teacher back at good old UB. I never ever suspected that you were gay."

"That's good," Dom said, "because I have always been in the closet at work. I made myself a promise that if I get a position down here, I'm going to be open and out, especially now that Tom is out at work."

"I always thought you were the best teacher I ever had at UB. Now you are going to be a neighbor. That's fantastic. Come here and give me a hug."

I excused myself and went inside to call Jake. "I'd like to ask Bob and Robert to join us tonight. I don't know if they will accept, but if they do can you increase our reservation. I'll drive them in my car and you can pick up Tom and Dom."

"Sure," Jake said. "Ask them, and if they accept, call me right back."

"Actually," Bob said, "we had plans for tonight, but I cancelled them. I didn't think Robert would be up to going out. I have a feeling that Robert would like us to join you fellows tonight." He looked at Robert who was nodding his assent.

Chapter Sixteen

During his interrogation of the students who were in the gym at the time of the shooting, one of them offered Mac this information providing that he would not reveal his source. Mac agreed. Four of the dead students were the four who beat up Johnny. Those four had asked him to join them, and thank God he had declined.

"Look," the boy said. "I've got a gay brother. He's the greatest guy in the world. His partner is a professional baseball player. I can't tell you who for obvious reasons. I really love both of them. I never cared that Johnny was gay, but they were always picking on him. The worst thing is that Mr. Sawyers, our gym teacher, actually egged them on. It's easy to see why Johnny went after the teacher too. I think the other victims were just in the wrong place at the wrong time."

"Thanks son," Mac said. "You have been a big help, and I promise not to reveal my source."

They shook hands and the youngster left. Mac wasn't sure why, but after that interview, he was able to find closure in both the hate crime and the school massacre, and he felt that he could now move on.

We had invited Izzy, Gloria, Marlene and Billy to dinner on the Friday night following the massacre. Jake was temporarily alone again, and he was joining us also. We asked Robert and Bob to stop in after dinner for dessert.

"I think your place is beautiful," Gloria said after I took her, Izzy and Billy on a tour. "I just love your view." They all fell in love with Jake too. He proudly dragged out pictures of Jonathan, and Gloria oohed and aahed.

The dinner went smoothly and I was pleased. I caught Izzy staring at Mac all through the evening. There was a look of admiration on his face, and I knew that he had definitely added Mac to his family, and maybe by extension, our son, Jake.

When they were leaving, Izzy took me aside. "Thank you, Wallie," he said. "I was right. You and Mac are terrific role models for Billy. I love you both." He kissed me on my cheek. Bob and Robert stayed awhile. They helped us clean up, and sat and chatted for some time before they went upstairs. After they left, Jake said, "Now can we cut the gab, and can you two guys continue my education, which is sorely lacking."

Mac laughed. "It's hardly lacking, young stud. You are an expert." The words weren't even out of Mac's mouth, and Jake was naked in our bed. I was next in because I still had my socks on, and took the time to remove them, so when Mac jumped in bed, he had to push me aside to get his tongue on Jake's delectable cock. To punish him, I climbed behind him and entered him with only spit for lubrication. I was amazed at how easily I went in. As Mac sucked Jake and I fucked him, I reached over Mac and grabbed his cock and started to stroke it. We all came fairly close together, laughing and giggling like the kids we were.

Somehow the days passed and it was time for Jonathan, Tom and Dominick to arrive for spring break. Mac called me at the office about 4 PM to inform me that he was in the middle of a murder investigation, and I would have to pick the guys up by myself. Izzy was in my office when I got the call, and he insisted on going with me. "I can't wait to give Tommy a great big hug and meet his college professor," he said. I didn't have the heart to turn him down.

Izzy took the commuter train with me and we picked up my car at the station. Driving to the airport I told Izzy that Jake's boyfriend was also coming in with Tom and Dom. "How wonderful for *my Jake,*" he said. MY JAKE? I was flabbergasted.

The first one I saw running to the security gate was Jonathan. He almost knocked me over in his enthusiastic greeting. I practically had to pull him off me.

"Izzy," I said, "this is Jake's partner Jonathan." Then in an effort to further impress my boss, I added. "He's studying engineering at UB."

Jonathan held out his hand, but Izzy embraced him in a bear hug. "It's wonderful to meet you," he said to Jonathan. "I already love Jake, so I can't exclude you." Jonathan was more than overwhelmed. Finally Tom and Dominick reached the gate. While Dominick embraced me and gave me a kiss on the lips, Tom wisely hugged Izzy and knocked the breath out of him. He then gave me a quick peck on a cheek, and said to Izzy, "I want you to meet Dominick. We've been together close to ten years."

Dominick and Izzy shook hands warmly and Izzy said to Tom, "Shame on you. All these years you kept this man out of my life, and in a way, you and Wallie lied to me. I would fire you both if I didn't love you like you were my own kids."

"We're both sorry, Izzy," I said. "First of all, neither of us had any idea about the other, and second of all, we were both afraid of how you would take it. You were pretty vocal about your displeasure with homosexuals."

"Pish tush," Izzy said. "You both know I'm not the most diplomatic person in the world, and if there's one thing you guys should have known is how much I love you. It wouldn't have made any difference in how I feel about you. Now, I called ahead, and Gloria is making dinner for all of us. No arguments! So let's get going."

On the way to Izzy's house, Izzy made Tom promise to come to the office Monday after house hunting, even if it was for just a little while. "Some vacation you gave me, boss," Tom joked.

When we got to Izzy's house, Gloria gushed over all of us and was truly happy to meet Dominick and Jonathan. Of course, she knew Tom. "Jonathan," she said. "You see that door over there. It leads to a small library. Open it up please."

Jonathan opened the door as if he expected a lion to jump out, and a lion did. Out jumped Jake, and wrestled Jonathan to the floor. "I called him right after Izzy called me," Gloria explained.

The two young men ate and ran. Jake had his car there, and they were free to go. "Don't be strangers," Gloria yelled after them. "Our door is always open."

We three stayed for a polite amount of time. Finally I suggested we go home so that Tom and Dominick could get some rest and steel themselves for a busy day of house hunting.

I was disappointed that Mac was not home when we arrived. I knew that he never answered his phone when he was working, so we would have to be patient and wait for his call. I got out of my work clothes, and stripped to my shorts. Tom and Dom got out of their travel clothes and also stripped to their shorts. I made coffee and we sat down in the living room waiting for Mac to call.

"I'll make it look good on Monday and I'll come into the office after lunch," Tom said. "I'll tell Izzy that we didn't look too hard, and we bought a mirror image of your apartment at the opposite end of the floor. I'll have to put some time in at the office, but if I remind him that I'm on vacation and want to show Dominick New York, he'll understand. Besides, I can play the religion card. This is Easter weekend."

"Dominick, you can use my car to go to your Brooklyn College interview on Monday. I'll write out driving directions for you," I said.

"I got directions on Mapquest," Dom answered. "I'd appreciate if you would verify them for me. You know, travel always poops me. I think I'll go to bed."

"Okay, honey," Tom agreed. "I'll be in soon."

"Let's all turn in," I said. "I have no way of knowing when Mac will get home."

As it turned out, he came home just before midnight. I was still awake in bed, watching a really old movie on TV. Mac leaned over me and kissed me tenderly.

"I love you," he said as if to reassure me.

"I love you more," I answered.

"Do you love me enough to make me a snack while I shower? I always feel so dirty after work."

"You've got it," I said. I jumped out of bed wearing only my birthday suit, and went into the kitchen. Thanks to Jake, we always have lots of deli in the fridge. I was preparing a roast beef sandwich when Tom came in the kitchen.

"What's going on?" he asked.

"Mac's home and I'm making him a sandwich," I answered.

"Hmmm! That looks good," Tom hummed.

"Sit," I said. "I'll make a sandwich for each of us. "How's Dom?"

"He's snoring happily away."

Mac joined us in a little while. He grabbed Tom and nearly broke his bones, hugging him so hard. The three of us enjoyed our repast, and finally we went to bed. When Tom and Dom woke up in the morning, Mac and I had already gone to work. I left a train schedule on the kitchen counter should Tom wish to follow through on his decision to come into the office after lunch.

Dominick scanned through our refrigerator and poured orange juice for the pair of them. He also made bacon and eggs with toast. After they cleaned up the kitchen, they showered. Of course they began to make love in the shower. They kissed and fondled, stroked and teased, until Dominick turned off the taps. "Let's get back in bed," he said. "We have all morning. In fact, we have all day if you change your mind about going into the office."

As soon as they got into bed, Dominick begged Tom to fuck him. Tom wasted no time, lubing his cock and Dom's ass. He entered Dominick with absolutely no resistance. "Go slow," Dom begged. Make it last as long as possible. This feels so good."

Tom lay as still as possible with Dominick lying on his stomach below him. "Yes, that's it," Dom said. "Try not to move."

They lay still like this for a very long time with Tom taking little nips of Dom's neck. "Thank you God," Tom whispered in Dom's ear.

"What are you thanking Him for?" Dominick asked.

"For you," Tom replied.

"You can fuck me now," Dominick advised Tom.

Tom came into the office at about 1:30 PM. The entire staff jumped up to greet him. Izzy was smiling from ear to ear. So, how did the house hunting go?" he asked.

"You and Wallie better sit down," Tom began his act. "Dominick and I wasted no time. We bought the first apartment we saw. Wallie, we're in 4J at the opposite end of the hall from you."

I screeched with joy, hoping that my acting was as good as Tom's.

"That's wonderful, wonderful. I'm so happy for you." Izzy said.

"Show Tom to the office we prepared for him, Wallie" Izzy said to me. "I know he's on vacation, so don't pass any work on to him, yet. But it wouldn't hurt to fill him in on some of our present projects."

I did just that, but of course, the two of us could not help ourselves. We immediately began to plan our marketing strategy. We got so lost in our work, we had no idea what time it was until I heard Izzy's voice. "Don't you two workaholics have people waiting for you at home? Before you go, here's a present. He handed Tom an envelope. "Here's tickets to two Broadway musicals. There are four tickets to each show so Wallie and Mac can go also."

Tom and I rushed out of the office. We missed my regular train, but the next one was only twenty minutes later. When I drove into the parking garage, I could see that Mac's car was already there. I felt the hood and it was still warm, so I knew that he had just come home.

When we entered the door, the apartment smelled like a wonderful Italian restaurant. The dining room table was set for six, and Dominick was putting the finishing touches to a gourmet meal.

"When you move in, I'll expect this every night," I laughed. "Where's Mac?"

"He's showering," Dom answered.

"I think I'll join him and change into something more comfortable," I said.

Tom added, "Me too. Change clothes, I mean."

While we were changing clothes, the doorbell rang. Dominick let Jake and Jonathan in. "Sorry we're late," Jonathan said. They all hugged each other and Dom assured them that they were not late.

Eating dinner that evening with my family, all the people in my life who I loved the most, I was filled once again with that euphoria of pure happiness. Then the cloud enveloped me. "It's too good to be true," I heard the voice of doom warning me. But at long last, I paid no attention!

Chapter Seventeen

On the evening before Billy's eighteenth birthday, Izzy made a big party at a local country club. He himself did not belong to the club, but he had a friend who did, and the friend arranged for Izzy to hold the party there. He made the party on Saturday instead of Sunday because Tom, Dom and Jonathan were leaving on a 7 PM flight on Sunday to return to Buffalo. They would not return again until the end of the semester.

The guest list included Izzy's immediate family (he had no others), Mac and I, Tom and Dominick, Jake and Jonathan and the rest of Izzy's office staff with their significant others. Billy, Jake and Jonathan had already agreed that Billy would drive over to their apartment early Sunday morning and they would see to it that when he went back to school on Monday, he would no longer be a virgin. Mac, I, Tom and Dom no longer needed to make "arrangements" for anything. We would be separated for another two and a half months, and we fully intended to enjoy each other in every combination after the party.

Dominick, the resident college professor, had suggested a list of items that Billy would find useful at the university in the fall, and we bought him birthday gifts from the list. The food at the club was delicious and the service was impeccable. Some of Billy's gifts were gag gifts and they got quite a laugh. Toward the end of the festivities Billy stood to thank everyone and then a strange and wonderful thing happened. Everyone looked into Billy's face and most of us could see what can only be described as a heavenly light shining from his eyes and it seemed to envelop his whole body. Izzy was standing close by his grandson. Suddenly his knees buckled, and he fell against Marlene who was standing next to him.

"Daddy," Marlene screamed, "Are you all right?"

"Didn't you see?" Izzy asked incredulously. "Eddie was standing with his arm around Billy. We don't ever have to worry about the boy again. His wonderful heroic father is his guardian angel."

Some of the guests thought that Izzy was losing it, but those of us who could see the light coming from the boy's eyes, and those of us who had even a smidgen of faith, knew that it was so. I leaned over and whispered in Mac's ear, "I want to go to church tomorrow, please." Mac nodded his head.

Tom had heard my plea. "Us too," he added.

On Sunday morning, before the sun came up, Billy was knocking on Jake's door. Jake was nude and half asleep when he answered the door.

"You've put me off long enough," Billy said. "This is it." Jake crept back into bed, and wrapped himself around Jonathan. Billy stripped and joined them. Neither Jake nor Jonathan had an exposed penis for Billy to play with, because they were mashed against each other, so Billy nested up against Jake's butt and waited for his lessons to begin. He actually fell asleep with his tutors.

An hour later, he was roused by a strange feeling. Something wet and hot was wrapped around his cock, and something hot and wet was caressing his balls. Jake and Jonathan had begun the lessons. After awhile they formed a daisy chain and sucked each other for a time. Then they changed positions so that a different cock was cradled in a different mouth. They were all too young to last too long, and they each had two orgasms in short order. They lay back on the bed, hugging and kissing each other until Billy said, "Please fuck me."

"Can you wait a few minutes?" Jake asked facetiously.

In our apartment, the four inhabitants had all slept in the king size master bed. We had sucked and fucked each other most of the night. Each of us came no less than twice, including Dominick. How we came, and who was the final recipient of our juices, I couldn't tell you. But one thing was for sure, it was with someone we loved. We finally fell asleep in a human heap at about 3 AM.

We had set the alarm for 8 AM so that we could all attend the Metropolitan Community Church in Manhattan. Dominick was Catholic and we others were of three different denominations of Protestant, so we felt that MCC was neutral territory and appropriate for all of us. The screeching alarm startled all of us, but we had made a commitment and we jumped out of bed. Mac and I showered in the master bath and Dom and Tom showered in the guest bath. We decided to have breakfast at the corner coffee shop before heading into the big city. We didn't want to take the time to cook and clean up afterwards.

We filed into the beautiful church and found seats together towards the rear. The service was nothing special until the pastor began to deliver his homily. Apparently, he believed in guardian angels that looked over us and kept us safe. He implored his flock to listen carefully for the angel voices when they were in a sticky situation, and the guidance would come. The four of us could hardly believe it, and I whispered to the others that when I said that I wanted to go to church last night, I could swear a voice told me to come here today. It was a bit frightening for all of us and yet we were awestruck by the whole experience.

Jake had to shoo a beaming, happy Billy out of his house late in the afternoon so that Jonathan could get ready for his flight back to Buffalo. Jake was driving him, Tom and Dominick to the airport at 5 PM to make their 7 PM flight. He felt that would leave enough time for heavy traffic and unexpected delays at security. Jake had to promise Billy that he would get together with him the following weekend for one on one further instruction.

When Jake arrived at the condo, Tom and Dom were waiting in the lobby. They had already said goodbye to Mac and me.

"Wallie wants to know if you are coming back here after you drop us off," Tom asked Jake.

"Maybe for a cup of coffee, but I'm too pooped for anything else."

"I take it that Billy is no longer a virgin," Dominick said.

"You take it correctly," Jonathan added.

Jake took out his cell phone and told Mac, who answered, that he would be back for a short visit in an hour or so. When he failed to show up in two hours, I began to worry and the feeling of dread came over me again. This time I vowed not to worry. There had to be an explanation. I kept trying to call Jake on his cell phone but he didn't answer.

At long last, our phone rang. It was Jake. He was in the airport with Jonathan, Tom and Dominick. There had been a terrible accident on the Grand

Central Parkway, and they had been stuck for almost two hours before the road could be cleared enough to start moving cars again. Unfortunately the guys had missed their flight, but they got rebooked on a flight leaving at 9:10 PM. Jake wanted to stay with Jonathan as long as possible, so he told us he would not visit us this evening.

After his call we were much relieved, and we finally thought about having some dinner. We hadn't been alone together since the beginning of spring break, and before that, Jake was apt to be sharing our bed, so Mac kept leering at me all through dinner.

"What?" I finally asked.

"You know what," he answered.

After our dinner plates were put into the dishwasher and the kitchen was cleaned, Mac took my hand and led us into our bedroom. When we got there, he started to strip me and I was totally compliant. When I was standing in front of him naked, he began to undress. I stood watching him as my desire erupted into flames. Mac pulled me into bed.

"What about a shower?" I asked.

"I don't want to waste time," he answered me. In an instant he was all over me, nipping and suckling every erogenous area I had on my body. It took awhile, but he finally started to suck my cock. His pace was slow. Long strokes of his tongue caressed the underside of my shaft. I began to moan in lustful pleasure as I came streaming into his mouth.

When I could breathe again, I said, "You know, honey, sometimes it's good, just the two of us." With that, I opened my night table and handed Mac a tube of KY Jelly. He knew just what to do, and once again, he brought me to glory as he shot his load, filling my insides with his precious nectar.

We were too exhausted to shower so I got us a towel to wipe up my jism, which had dribbled out of Mac's mouth, and Mac's jism, which had dribbled out of my ass. We lay on our backs, holding hands, and started to drift off, satisfied and happy. I must have just fallen asleep when the phone rang. It was Jake, who just wanted to tell us that they had taken off at last, and he had just gotten home. We thanked him for letting us know and we fell asleep.

During the previous week, Dominick had been offered a position at both Brooklyn and Queens Colleges. He was hard pressed to make a choice. Queens was closer to home, but Brooklyn's campus looked very much like an Ivy League school. He knew several professors at Brooklyn, having worked with them in the past. In the end, he flipped a coin and CUNY Brooklyn was his choice.

The time seemed to drag, but finally the semester ended. We attended Billy's graduation along with Jake. Billy received several honors and scholarships. When he got up to deliver the valedictory, his body was enveloped by that indescribable light. I clearly heard several people gasp when they saw him. All I could think of was that Billy was destined for great things. I had no doubt that he would find a cure for cancer or some other incurable disease.

Jonathan moved home, and Jake put him to work in the store until the fall semester would begin. Tom and Dominick moved in to our building, to our utter delight, and Dom immediately got an evening summer job teaching English as a second language two nights a week. He wasn't even unpacked yet, when he and Tom got subscriptions to the Metropolitan Opera and the New York City Ballet for the upcoming fall season. Mac and I declined the offer to join them, but we were thrilled to see how happy Dominick was. It wasn't that we lacked any culture, but Mac's hours were so unpredictable, that we just couldn't commit to a subscription.

We all settled into a routine. Every Saturday night we went to dinner and a floor show in Greenwich Village. Bob and Robert joined Mac and me, Tom and Dom, and Jake and Jonathan. We were an inseparable family group, but during the week, we were busy doing our own things. We all spoke constantly on the phone during the week, but pretty much did not socialize until the weekend.

Since our experience at Billy's birthday party, we had taken to going to MCC every Sunday morning, and that included all eight of us. Even though Billy was not physically present, whenever I was in the church, I felt the presence of some unknown force enveloping all of us. I became convinced that Billy's hero father was protecting the eight of us. Little by little, I got over the feeling that my life was too good to be true. I came to realize that I was a good person, and I began to love myself. Then I was able to accept the fact that I deserved what I had.

Tom and I somehow found ourselves on the church's publicity committee, and we produced ads for the local gay media promoting the church. Through our ads we let the gay community know what great outreach programs were available through the church. I came to believe that Billy and his father had come into my life as messengers of God, and I was no longer a skeptic.

In fact, yet another miracle was about to occur as further proof that Eddie was looking after his son, Billy.

Jake and Jonathan volunteered to drive Billy to the University and help him settle in. The night before his departure, Billy said his goodbyes to his mother and to his grandparents. Marlene drove him to Jake's apartment with all his suitcases, his laptop, and other essentials. As soon as she left, my sons gave Billy quite a sendoff. They blew his mind that night with sex and love that he would remember forever. They started the drive to Binghamton at 4:30 AM. By 8 AM they were almost there and they finally stopped for breakfast.

They arrived at the University at 10:00 AM and sought out Billy's dorm room. They helped him unpack, set up his computer and put all his clothes neatly in the dresser and the closet provided to him.

"We'd like to stay and meet your roommate," Jake said, "but I want to be home before dark so we are going to take off. You're on your own now, you young adult." They hugged and kissed and Jake and Jonathan hurried out so that Billy would not see the tears in their eyes. "We'll see you at Thanksgiving," Jonathan yelled as they left.

After they left, Billy found the cafeteria and had a light lunch. He returned to his room to find his new room mate just moving in. He was being helped by his father.

"Hi," Billy said, "I'm Bill Campbell." He stuck out his hand, and his room mate grabbed it.

"Nice to meet you," the young man said. "I'm Brandon Galen and this is my dad, Randy."

"Can I help you?" Billy offered.

"You know," Randy said, "That would be real nice. It would give you two guys a chance to get acquainted and I could head for home and get there at a decent hour."

"Where's home?" Billy asked.

"Bowmansville, just outside of Buffalo," Randy answered. He extended his hand to Billy. "Really nice to have met you," he said. Then he took hold of Brandon and gave him a real hard bear hug and ran from the room."

"You're lucky to have a dad," Billy said. "My dad was killed in Iraq almost three years ago, but I know he's always around looking after me."

"Then you're luckier than I am," Brandon commented.

Billy was disturbed by that remark but decided to ignore it. "My grandpa makes up for my not having a dad," Billy informed Brandon. "He spoils me rotten and he's always there for me. Besides him, I have a bunch of guys in my life who look after me like I was the second coming or something. Sometimes it's embarrassing."

"I've got a grandfather also," Brandon said. "I have no idea where he is. Nobody in the family is allowed to speak about him. Apparently my grandma caught him cheating on her. She's dead now, and my dad and his sister never speak of him. They won't forgive him and they won't look for him. I've been tempted to seek him out," Brandon concluded.

"That would be a really forgiving thing to do," Billy said. "It also sounds like a fun thing to do. I wouldn't mind helping out. We could do a computer search."

"We'll see about it," Brandon said. The two young men then went about setting up their room exactly as they would like it to be.

"What's your major?" Brandon asked.

"I'm pre-med," Billy answered.

"No shit! So am I. Do you have your class schedule handy?" The boys dug their schedules out of their newly organized desks, and discovered that they were in every class together.

"How neat is that?" Billy asked.

"We can really study together," Brandon added.

The room mates then began to talk about their hopes and aspirations for the future. In no time they were conversing like two old friends, and before they knew it, the room was darkening and evening was coming on.

"Care for some dinner?" Billy asked. "I've already discovered the cafeteria."

"After dinner," Brandon asked. "Do you think we should check out the student union?"

"You can, if you would like, but I got up at 3:30 AM this morning and I'm ready for the sack. I'll take a rain check."

"OK," Brandon said. "I'll try not to wake you when I get in."

After dinner Billy went back to his room and retrieved his bathroom kit. He also took a towel to the shower room. He showered and shaved to save time in the morning. He wrapped the towel around him and went back to his room. He hung the towel on a rack in his room and put his dirty underwear in a laundry bag. He was just getting a fresh pair of briefs from his dresser when Brandon came in trying to be as quiet as he could.

"Oops! Sorry," he said.

"Think nothing of it," Billy said. He, Jake and Jonathan walked around naked all the time so he could talk like a big shot. "We were bound to see each other naked sooner or later. In fact at home I sleep in the nude."

"So do I," Brandon said. "I don't see any reason to change that. Do you?"

"If it's OK with you, it's OK with me."

"You look fresh showered," Brandon remarked.

"I usually shower in the morning, but I figured the place would be a madhouse in the morning so I just showered now."

"Good idea. I think I'll do the same." Brandon stripped naked, and of course Billy checked him out. He was cut and about the same size as Billy. No competition here. Brandon wrapped a towel around himself and took off to the showers. When he returned, the lights were still on in the room and Billy was sound asleep. He was sleeping above his blanket and was lying on his back. He was fully exposed to Brandon.

Before he shut the lights, Brandon looked longingly at Billy, and had to restrain himself from stroking Billy's cock. He got into bed and fell asleep, imagining what it would be like to be sucking Billy's beautiful cock. He tight shut his eyes so that he could picture the scene more vividly. As a result he failed to see the light between the two beds. The angel blessed both young men and watched over them all night.

They had arrived on a Saturday. Orientation was on Monday morning. They had the whole day Sunday to do whatever they wanted to do so neither was in a hurry to get out of bed. When he woke up, Brandon looked over at Billy and asked, "Are you awake?"

"Yes. I'm just too lazy to get out of bed."

"Me too."

"Want to do something today?" Billy asked.

"Yeah! Let's go into town, have brunch and check out the amenities."

"Wonderful idea." Billy said and jumped out of bed. His morning woodie was waving in Brandon's face and Brandon nearly swooned. He wondered how he could get through the year with such a beautiful, off limits cock, staring him in the face. What would he have done if he knew that Billy was thinking the same thing?

"I gotta pee," Billy said.

"Me too."

They each put on a pair of briefs, which did not hide their erections, and ran to the bathroom.

When they got back to their room, Brandon said seriously, "Bill I have to ask you something. Would you mind terribly if we didn't sleep naked? Could we wear underwear?"

"Sure, but why?"

Brandon's face turned very red. He tried to talk but couldn't.

"What?" Billy asked.

"Bill, I'm gay and seeing you naked is too much. It's turning me on and making me wish for things, I can't have." He buried his face in his hands, afraid to look at Billy. He certainly was not expecting what happened next. Billy knelt down in front of him and removed Brandon's hands from his face. He leaned into Brandon and kissed him full on the lips.

Brandon was speechless. "It's going to be one hell of a year." Billy said. "Are you a virgin?"

"Yes," Brandon said sadly.

"I have much to teach you and you have much to learn," Billy said very seriously.

Chapter Eighteen

All plans previously made regarding going into the city to have brunch and checking out the amenities, were abandoned. Instead the two freshmen locked their door, drew the blinds in their room, and quickly stripped naked. Brandon was shaking like a leaf.

"What's wrong?" the more experienced Billy asked him.

"Nothing, nothing at all. I'm just so happy. First of all I've got a great room mate like you, and secondly I find out he's gay. I can't believe my good fortune. Last night when I came from the showers and saw you lying there, naked and inviting, it was all I could do not to touch you. Your body was glowing and I had a desire to wrap myself around you and absorb that glow. It was the strangest feeling."

"Feel free to wrap yourself around me now," Billy invited Brandon.

"Enough small talk. Let me show you what my two fantastic teachers taught me. We'll start with oral sex and then when you have mastered that, I'll take you into anal sex. That's the best, the only real male sex, as far as I am concerned," Billy told Brandon. "Lie back," he then commanded.

Brandon lay down on his back. His throbbing cock was waving at the ceiling as Billy lay down on top of him and began a one hour trip around the world. Brandon alternately sighed, moaned and cried until he could bear it no longer, and he begged Billy to bring him to orgasm. Billy took Brandon's cock deep into his throat and caressed it lovingly with his tongue and lips. In no time at all, Brandon's juices flowed. His jism was so plentiful that the two young men were able to share it between them.

"I need to catch my breath," Brandon said, "and then I'll do it to you."

"Don't sweat it," Billy said. "We have all the time in the world. Let's just talk while you recover."

"First of all," Brandon said, "thank you for giving me my first experience. I will remember this moment for as long as I live. You really seem to know what you are doing. I'll bet you have been with dozens of guys."

"No, just two guys, my brothers."

Brandon gasped. "Your brothers?"

Billy laughed. "Not my blood brothers, goofball. My gay brothers." Billy then went on to tell Brandon about Tom and Wallie who worked for his grandfather. "They are both gay, and Grandpa asked them to mentor me and help me deal with school bullies." Tom and Wallie have partners, and the two couples consider themselves to be brothers. They have united as a gay family. Wallie met a young student some time ago, and they became great friends. Jonathan, the student, has a partner, Jake, who is a business man, and Tom and Wallie adopted them as their sons.

"Recently, a couple who live in the condo where Tom, Dominick, Mac and Wallie live, were added to the family. Then, when I turned eighteen, Jake and Jonathan adopted me as their gay brother. In summary, Mac, Wallie, Tom, Dominick, Bob and Robert are brothers. Mac and Wallie are fathers to me, Jake and Jonathan, so their brothers are our uncles. Get it?"

"I get it," Brandon said, "but it will take time for me to learn all these names. You still haven't told me how you got to be so experienced."

"I was a virgin right up to my eighteenth birthday. I pleaded with Jake and Jonathan to remedy that, but they wouldn't touch me until I was legal. I spent my birthday in bed with them. Learning was never such pleasure, or so much fun. Then when Jonathan went back to college, Jake continued to instruct me one on one. I hope I can teach you everything they taught me."

Let's see how I am doing so far," Brandon said and he threw himself on top of Billy. Billy thought that his room mate did very well for the first time, but he did have to warn him about teeth a few times. They sucked each other alternately for a few hours, missing lunch completely. As it grew dark, Billy suggested they go to the cafeteria for dinner. There was still so much they wanted to learn about one another. They found a rare table for two in a corner and ate dinner alone.

Billy spoke first. He had been an army brat for many years and then his father, Colonel Edward Campbell, was deployed to Iraq. He and four of his men were killed there. His mother moved them back to Long Island so she could be near her parents. She got her real estate license, and that's how she met his two dads, Mac and Wallie. They were looking for a condo. "She actually asked them to mentor me. She believed that I could not have better role models. Mac is a police detective and Wallie works for my Grandpa in marketing."

Brandon listened intently. "Did your dad know that you were gay?" he asked.

"We never spoke of it, but I am sure he suspected. Before he left for Iraq he asked me if there was anything I wanted to tell him. I didn't tell him then, and I'm sorry to this day. I dream sometimes that I told him and that he assured me that it made absolutely no difference to how much he loved me. I really would like to believe that."

Brandon sighed. "Well you sure have a great support system. I wish I had it. I'd love to meet your dads, uncles and brothers. I'll bet they make you feel safe and protected."

"That they do! That they do. But you sound as if you are all alone in the world," Billy observed.

"I am."

"Don't your folks know that you are gay?" Billy wanted to know.

"Are you kidding? My dad is one of the most homophobic men I have ever met in my life. Let me tell you something. Remember I told you that my grandmother caught my grandfather cheating on her. I neglected to tell you that he was with a man. She kicked him out of the house, and took him for all he had. He faithfully continued to support my dad and my aunt through college and beyond, but they would never speak to him or forgive him. I can remember my dad sounding off against queers every time there was an incident in the paper or if they rallied for gay rights. You should hear him rant about gay marriage."

Brandon paused and Billy decided to say nothing until he was ready to continue.

"I was raised hearing all about queers and faggots and their destinies in hell. This was kind of funny since my dad never sets foot in a church. He hates my grandfather so much, he even changed our surname. When I began to realize that I was gay, I wanted to kill myself. Actually if I told my dad, he would probably do the killing for me."

"You don't know that," Billy said. My grandfather was the same way, but when he found out that Wallie, Tom and I were gay, he made a complete turn around. He knew us and loved us. We were no longer abstract sinners, and he could not be more supportive to me, and my whole gay family."

"I wish I could believe that about my father, but you have never seen the hatred in his eyes. Besides, my grandfather was not abstract, and he has never forgiven him."

After dinner they returned to their room, stripped, and took showers together. They were very discreet in case someone might join them. Back in their room, they held each other tightly as their cocks rubbed fiercely against each other.

"Let's rest tonight," Billy said. "You really knocked me out today. I'll continue the lessons tomorrow evening."

"That's fine, but I'd really like to sleep with you tonight," Brandon said.

"I wouldn't have it any other way." They lay entwined together in Billy's bed and Billy asked, "What was your surname before your dad changed it?"

"Gallini," Brandon answered.

Billy pulled away from Brandon and sat bolt upright in bed. "What's wrong?" Brandon asked.

"What was your grandfather's name?"

"Dominick, I believe. Why are you asking?"

"Brandon, don't get too excited until I verify all this, but I think your grandfather is one of my gay uncles."

"Don't get excited! Are you kidding? I need him so badly. I need an ally when my dad finds out."

"From what you tell me, Uncle Dom is not going to be much of an ally, but we need to find out," Billy said. "What time is it?"

"9:45! Why?"

"It's early enough to call him."

Billy got out his cell phone and found Tom and Dominick in his speed dial. Tom answered the phone.

"I'm glad it's you, Uncle Tom. Listen, I think that Uncle Dominick's grandson is my room mate. Do you know what Uncle Dominick's son's name is?"

Tom was hyperventilating when he answered. "I'm sure it's Randy. About ten years ago Dom hired a detective to locate his family. He didn't want to contact them, but he wanted to make sure they were all right. Randy had a wife named Rhonda, a son, Brandon and a daughter, Sarah."

Billy was speechless, but he mustered himself and said, "Uncle Tom, Brandon is my room mate. What are we going to do about it?"

"When is your last class on Friday?"

"We are free at 3 PM."

Check the bus schedule and get your asses home. I'm not telling Dom. I'll have your dad's make a party in their apartment and we'll surprise him."

"Hold on," Billy said and he went to get a bus schedule he had picked up somewhere. "The 3:30 bus makes only one stop in Monticello and gets in to the Port Authority at 8:15."

"I'll have Jake pick you up so you don't waste time on the railroad and Dominick won't suspect anything. You can go to your dads' apartment and they'll let us know when you are there. Then I'll bring old grandpa over. OH MY GOD," Tom said.

"What's the matter?" Billy asked.

"What if Brandon doesn't want to meet Dominick."

"Oh, he does, Uncle Tom, he does. You see he's gay. Besides, my dad, my real dad, arranged the whole thing, and please don't comment on that or ask me how I know. I just know. "

When he finally and reluctantly hung up the phone, Billy rushed to Brandon who was sobbing softly. He put his arms around his room mate to comfort him and Brandon said, "I don't want to wait until tomorrow for more lessons. I need it now.'

Billy went to his dresser and took out a tube of lube. "I didn't know how lucky I would be," he said, "so I came to school prepared. I've been more than lucky." He lay down on his back and began to grease his asshole.

"Come here," he said quietly to Brandon. When Brandon came close, Billy greased Brandon's hard cock and placed it at the opening in his crack. "My brothers and I usually rim each other before this point, but I think you need this badly." He placed Brandon's head against his hole and helped Brandon push it in.

When Brandon had entered Billy fully, he sighed. "This is so much better than my fantasies," he said. He started to pump and Billy pumped with him all the while contracting and then loosening his ass hole.

"Is it too early to tell you that I love you?" Brandon asked.

"I don't think so. I fell in love with you when I walked into our room."

Billy and Brandon sat on the bus counting off the miles. *How could one mile take so long?* Billy thought. Brandon was nervous and fidgety and he started to bite his nails so Billy took his hands in his and prevented him from doing any more damage.

"I'm scared," Brandon said.

"You don't have to be," Billy assured him. "Your grandfather is one of God's saints. You two are going to love each other immediately. I assure you. Besides this whole reunion was heaven made."

The bus was dark so Billy laid his palm on Brandon's crotch and stroked slowly. This did indeed help Brandon to relax.

They got off the bus with only carry on bags. A handful of people were waiting on the platform. Billy spotted Jonathan immediately and ran to him. They kissed on the lips not caring who saw. Brandon realized pangs of jealousy, but when Billy introduced them, Jonathan embraced Brandon and kissed him on the lips also. Brandon looked surprised so Jonathan said, "Tom indicated that there might be something going on between you guys so that makes you my brother and that's what brothers do."

Brandon laughed and gave Jonathan another kiss.

"Where's Jake?" Billy asked.

"It's tough for him to get away from the store on Friday evenings, but he'll be at our dads' place shortly. Now let's get going."

"Who will be there?" Billy asked.

"Your mom and grandparents and *"the family."* When he said, *"the family"* both young men knew exactly who he meant.

When they got into Jonathan's car, Billy insisted that Brandon sit up front and he sat in the back. As soon as they were on their way he called Wallie.

"Hi pop. We're just leaving the port authority terminal and traffic looks light. I hope Dominick doesn't have a heart attack."

"Well, there's a doctor on the third floor and I saw him come home when I did. How's school so far?"

"It's great. I'll tell you all about it later. We're going to stay with Uncle Tom and Brandon's grandpa." Wallie thought that it was strange that he didn't say Uncle Dominick like he always did. Then he realized that if Dom was Brandon's grandfather, maybe he was Billy's also, by injection.

Jonathan was lucky enough to find street parking not far from the building entrance. He had a key to the lobby and let them in. They hurried into Wallie's and Mac's apartment. Billy was devoured by his mother and grandparents. He introduced them to Brandon, and Izzy said, "He looks just like his grandfather. I could pick him out in a lineup."

Then he introduced him to the rest of the family, while Jonathan called Tom and told him to come over. The apartment became as quiet as a tomb since nobody was talking. Emotion and expectancy had taken over. Then they heard the light tap on the door. "Come in," Mac said.

Dominick froze in a state of shock when he saw all these people. "My God," he said. "Is it someone's birthday? I know it isn't mine." Then he spotted Billy and ran and embraced him. "What are you doing home? I hope you haven't quit school," he said jokingly.

"Not at all, Uncle Dom," Billy said. "I'd like you to meet someone who has come to mean a great deal to me. It's my room mate and my lover."

Dom looked at Brandon and got concerned. The lad looked like he was going to faint. "Are you all right?" he asked Brandon. Brandon just kept on staring at his grandfather.

Uncle Dom," Billy said, "my room mate's name is Brandon Gallini." He didn't say Galen to avoid confusion and to let it all sink in. Dom's legs gave out and Tom and Billy caught him. He stood back up on his feet. Tears filled his eyes so that he could not see, but he held out his arms and Brandon fell into them. Grandson and grandfather stood wrapped in each other's arms crying like babies. So was everybody else.

"I've wanted to look for you for years, Grandpa, but I was afraid of what my father would do. I'm scared to death to tell him I'm gay."

"Please don't be afraid. You'll see. He'll still love you. He just lashed out at me because I betrayed his mother. I have never forgiven myself for that either, but I had no choice."

"I know. I know," Brandon reassured Dominick.

"The private detective told me that Randy changed his name to Galen," Dom said.

"He did," Uncle Dom. I just wanted to make sure you knew who this was and what a miracle we are witnessing." As Billy said these words, I swear I could see his body glowing. Izzy told me on Monday morning at the office that he actually saw Eddie standing in a corner smiling. "I'm getting used to it," he said very matter of factly, "I don't faint anymore."

Around about 1 AM the party began to break up. Izzy, Gloria and Marlene went home. They understood that Billy wanted to spend the weekend with Brandon, and that Brandon wanted to spend it with Dominick so they did not object.

Bob and Robert went upstairs, Jake and Jonathan decided to spend the night with Mac and me, and Billy and Brandon traipsed up the hall to Dominick's place.

When Dominick entered his apartment he collapsed on the sofa and started to cry. "It's a miracle!" he kept repeating over and over. Brandon sat down next to him and put his arm around Dominick's shoulder. Tom motioned for Billy to come into the kitchen so they could be alone.

"Please don't cry Grandpa," Brandon said. "We're going to be all right."

Dominick placed Brandon's head on his chest. "Listen to me, my darling grandson. You must be brave and tell your father that you are gay. Don't live a lie and ruin your life like I did, and even like Wallie did for too long. I promise you his anger is against me. He will always love you. I know this to be truth. And God forbid, if he rejects you, well, I paid for his support and his education long after I had to, and if he won't do as much for you, then I will. You have nothing to worry about, and I urge you to tell the truth. Also he will love Billy too. There is something spiritual about that boy. When I am with him, I often feel that there is an angel in the room."

"I know, Grandpa," Brandon said. "I can actually see his body glowing and when I make love to him it's like a spiritual happening. I love him Grandpa, and I think he loves me too."

"Of course he does. I can see the way he looks at you. Now I think we should all get some sleep. You guys sleep as long as you want tomorrow. We're all going out to dinner and a show tomorrow evening like we do every Saturday."

"Grandpa," Brandon said. "I'm going to call my father tomorrow and tell him. I want to do it while you are around. I need your strength and your support and maybe I need you to pick up the pieces."

Chapter Nineteen

Dominick took his grandson and Billy directly to the guest room. "Are you boys tired?" he asked.

"No," Brandon answered for both of them. "We're too excited. We are excited that we found you, and we are excited that we found each other."

"Good," Dominick said. "Let's go in the kitchen. I'll make some hot chocolate and I've got some doughnuts. I want you to tell me everything I've missed all these years."

Tom made the chocolate and Billy set the table. Dom and Brandon sat down at the table, and Brandon began to talk. The other three listened in rapt attention.

His dad was a prosecuting attorney for the city of Buffalo, and his aunt was a school teacher in Amherst, a suburb of Buffalo. She never married and had no children. His mother Rhonda managed the lingerie department at a Walmart in Bowmansville. His sister Sarah was a knockout and a cheerleader. She was in her junior year in high school. Randy was very homophobic. He was always on scene to protest any demonstrations in favor of gay rights. Brandon was truly afraid that he would not see his family again, if he came out to his father. But he concluded, "I'm not so scared anymore. I've got Bill now and a whole new family I can rely on. I feel protected and insulated already."

"You can say that again," Tom said, by way of an 'amen.'

They talked for over two hours with both Dominick and Brandon crying intermittently. Finally Tom said, "We better get to bed. Tomorrow is another big day. We'll be going out for dinner and a show. Let's just sleep in and save our energies for the evening."

The two couples retired to their respective bedrooms. By now Billy was comfortable with his adopted family so he never bothered to close the bedroom door. It didn't much matter. Everyone was so tired that although they were each naked, they fell asleep immediately.

Tom and Dominick slept until eight, which was late for them, but they stayed in bed so as not to wake the boys. They began to play and fondle and before they knew it, they were ready for sex. They didn't even bother to shower or brush there teeth. They were engaged in a passionate game of sixty-nine, when Billy stirred. He could see right across the hall to their room. He wasn't embarrassed, but he thought that Brandon might be if he saw his grandfather actually having sex. He crept out of bed and silently closed the door. Then he got back in bed and snuggled against Brandon who was still peacefully asleep.

Billy couldn't sleep. Brandon was still sleeping so Billy crept out of bed and went to the bathroom. He relieved himself from both ends, brushed his teeth and started the taps in the shower. Just as he stepped in, Brandon grabbed him around the waist.

"Brush your teeth and do whatever else you have to do," Billy said. "I'll wait for you in the shower." Brandon rushed through his morning routines and bounded into the shower.

"I'm so happy," he said as he began to soap Billy's back. "In my whole life I can't remember being this happy. Even if my father disowns me, I've got a ready made family." He turned Billy around and started kissing him so passionately that Billy had to lean against the wall to keep from falling. They didn't even want to have sex. They just wanted to dress and spend the day with their family.

They weren't supposed to be anywhere this weekend but in Buffalo, so Billy's mother and grandparents had reluctantly agreed to pretend that the boys were not at home, and they promised not to call them or bother them. Marlene was cool with that, but at 9 AM Izzy called Billy.

"I swear I won't bother you," he said, "but if you need something, just call me, and I'll take care of it 'toot sweet.'" Izzy loved the French expression for pronto.

"I love you too, Grandpa," Billy said and hung up laughing.

The four of them were joined by Bob, Robert and me at the corner coffee shop for breakfast. Mac, Jake and Jonathan had to work until mid afternoon. The mood was light and joyous. Everyone kept hugging Brandon and Dominick and congratulating them on the miracle of their discovering each other. Then Brandon's phone rang. It was his father.

"Dad," Brandon said, "I'm out to breakfast with a gang of guys. It's too noisy here. Can I call you back in an hour or so?"

"Make it before noon," Randy said. Your mother and I have to go out then."

The mood suddenly became more serious. The family grew quiet and Brandon was prompted to say, "Grandpa, when breakfast is done, I'd like to go back to your apartment and call my father."

"Sure," Dominick said. "Sure."

Brandon went into the guest room alone, and closed the door. Randy picked up on the first ring. "Hi son," he said. "I just wanted to find out how your first week away from home went."

"Great, Dad, great. So much has happened that I don't know where to begin."

"Well, let's hear it. I'm all ears," Randy said enthusiastically.

"First of all, Bill and I hit it off great. I can see our friendship lasting forever. His father is some sort of war hero. He was killed in Iraq."

"I am so sorry to hear that," Randy interjected. "I could tell that he came from good stock."

"Anyway," Brandon continued. "We were sitting around talking and telling each other all about one another, and I don't know why, but I told Bill about Grandpa. Bill then told me that his uncle had a friend, who originally came from Buffalo, and their stories were the same. I told him grandpa's name and Billy called his uncle. To cut to the chase, Dad, Grandpa is Billy's uncle's life partner."

There was utter silence on the other end, forcing Brandon to continue his narrative. "Actually, Dad," he added, Billy's uncle is not his real uncle. He's his gay uncle. He's part of a large gay family."

This time there was no silence from Randy. "Are you telling me that your fucking room mate is gay? I'll see to it that you are transferred out of that room immediately. I don't want you contaminated by a family of fags."

Brandon winced.

"I'm not finished," he said. "Please hear me out. I came into New York last night with Bill and I met Grandpa. We spent the night at his condo."

Dead silence, so Brandon continued. "Dad, Grandpa may be the only real family I have left after I tell you that I am gay. I've always been gay and I always will be gay. I won't let you separate me from Bill. I love him."

"I'll cut you off," Randy screeched. "You'll have to leave college."

"So be it, Dad. I am what I am. All I know is that since I met Bill, I have never been happier in my life. You disowned Grandpa, but he never disowned you. He provided for you until you could take care of yourself. You can disown me if you like, but that makes Grandpa a bigger man than you are.

"How dare you talk to me like that," Randy screamed. "You're not welcome in my home anymore. You're over eighteen and I am emancipating you. If you want to rot in hell, that's fine with me."

"Sorry Dad, you're way off base. Bill has a guardian angel, who brought us together, and brought Grandpa into my life. I can actually see the celestial light surrounding Bill. Examine your un-Christian like hatred of God's creations. I think it's you who might rot in hell. But I forgive you and I'll always be ready to welcome you into my arms. I know that Grandpa feels the same way."

Randy hung up the phone with such ferocity, that Brandon's ear hurt. He went out to the living room where Dominick, Tom and Billy were waiting. The others and I had discreetly gone home. Brandon was expressionless. The other men could not read his emotions. "Well, Grandpa," he said. "We are both officially disowned, and I am officially emancipated."

Dominick grabbed Brandon and held him tight. "Listen, *my son*," he said. "Now that you are emancipated, I'll call the right people at the university and see what scholarship grants are available to you. Whatever else is needed, I will take care of it for you. I'll see to it that you get the best education in the country. Promise me you won't worry."

"Hey, don't leave me out," Tom said to Brandon. "I'm your grandfather-in-law, and I will see to it that your education is not lacking as well." That having been said, the four of them engaged in a group hug. They were totally unaware that they were surrounded by a glow of such warmth and beauty, that not even a renaissance artist could have captured it.

When they pulled apart, Brandon said, "I have been so afraid of my father all my life, that I really didn't think that I loved him. Suddenly, I feel sorry for him and I realize that I do love him."

"We'll all pray for him," Tom promised.

"Please don't worry about me. I am so happy I can barely handle it." He grabbed Billy's hand and added, "Thank you God. Thank you, angel of

God, for bringing Bill, my Grandfather and all these wonderful people into my life. I have a family at last."

The family turned their Saturday night dinner and show into a big celebration. They all laughed their sides off when the management carded Jake and Jonathan as well as Billy and Brandon. Brandon and Dominick sat across the table from each other. Their eyes danced and smiled, and unspoken words flew across the table. "I love you," they silently communicated to each other. Whether the show that night was good or bad, it didn't matter. The family all thought it was the greatest show that they had ever seen.

Brandon and Billy were due to leave for Binghamton at 5 PM on Sunday. The one-stop bus would get them in at 9:30. Everyone in the family slept late Sunday morning. There had been much love making during the night. They were stuffed from the meal that they had eaten the night before and agreed to go directly to church, have lunch out, and then hang out with the boys until it was time to take them to the bus station. Of course, Tom and Dominick insisted on being the one's to take them there.

As usual, when something occurred in their lives, good or bad, the pastor's homily seemed directed straight at the family. This morning, the subject of his sermon was 'forgiveness.' He spoke of a young man who had been disowned and rejected by his family after he came out to them. The young man came to his pastor for guidance. The pastor advised the young man to forgive his family. He told him that it was necessary to forgive them and cleanse himself of all the hate they were sending to him. Free of guilt and their hatred, he would then be able to send them his love whenever he thought of them, and move on with his life. The pastor assured the young man that he could not go on grieving and feeling guilty if he was to have a full and productive life. "Forgiveness is the way of the savior," he said. His final words were, "By the way, that young man was me."

Dominick and Brandon were squeezing each other's hands and sobbing softly. Tom put his arm around Dom's shoulder and Billy did the same for Brandon.

As the years passed, wonderful things happened: Dominick introduced Marlene to a widower who taught with him at Brooklyn College, and she remarried. Izzy retired and left the business to his staff. Tom and I got the controlling shares, so for all intents and purposes it was our business. Mac became the Chief of Police of Nassau County, NY. Bob and Robert each became the principals of their high schools, and, with Mac's help, they both started policies of zero tolerance for bullying at their schools. Jonathan landed a great job with the City of New York as a Civil Engineer. Jake expanded his business and now owns four delicatessens throughout Long Island.

But it was Billy who fulfilled the promise we all had expected of him. I can only thank God that Izzy and Gloria lived to see the honors which befell him. In their thirty-sixth year, Billy and his life partner, Brandon, jointly created a drug which destroyed cancer cells before they could multiply. The drug acted like synthetic white blood cells and devoured everything foreign to the body that it came in contact with. Two years later, using the principals they had developed with the first drug, they altered the drug so that it prevented cancer cells from ever developing in the body at all. It could be administered easily and safely as a vaccine to prevent every sort of cancer. For this accomplishment they were jointly awarded The Nobel Prize for medicine. I thought back to Billy's high school graduation and I remembered distinctly that I had predicted this miraculous medical discovery. The angel must have spoken to me!

When the two doctors won the Nobel Prize, Brandon received a telegram from his father. It simply said, "Congratulations!" Brandon took that as an invitation and called his parents' home. Unfortunately his father hung up on him.

It was one of life's ironies that Dom developed pancreatic cancer before his grandsons' miracle came to be. We lost him all too soon. Tom had always prepared himself for this event, since Dominick was so much older than he. Still the loss of his beloved partner was difficult for him to bear. Mac introduced Tom to a fellow police officer with whom he had become very friendly. Bob introduced him to a couple of school teachers he thought would be a good match. Actually Tom became friends with all of them, and he admitted to being a fuck buddy to all of them, but he wasn't ready to commit.

After Dominick's death, Tom renewed his subscription to the opera, but dropped his ballet subscription. It was difficult to attend his first opera as a single, but he vowed to see it through. He was reading the playbill and wondering who would take the seat he had given up, when a gentleman excused himself, stepped over Tom and sat down in what had been Dominick's seat. Tom overcame any shyness he may have had because his curiosity got the best of him. He took a good look at the gentleman. He was about five years younger than Tom, and about two inches shorter. He was very good looking and when he removed his coat, Tom could see that he worked out and had a good body. His gaydar was totally unrevealing.

"Hi," Tom said cheerily. "Do you have a subscription or are you here for tonight's performance only?"

"I have a subscription," the man answered. "I just moved here from Syracuse. I was lucky to get such a good seat, but they told me that it just became available."

Tom stuck out his hand. "I'm Tom," he said. "I have a subscription also so we'll be seeing a lot of each other."

The man took Tom's hand and returned a firm grip. "It's nice to meet you," he said. "I'm Fred. Like I said, my firm transferred me and I've only been here two weeks. I couldn't afford Manhattan housing so I took a place in Queens."

"How did you get here?" Tom asked. "Did you drive or use the subway?"

"Subway!" Fred answered. I'm still a little frightened of driving in New York."

"I live in Valley Stream. I go through Queens on my way home. If you are on my way, I could drive you home after the opera," Tom offered the stranger. Then he wondered why he did that. He didn't know the guy and couldn't tell if he was straight or gay. He only knew that he liked Fred the moment he saw him.

The house lights began to dim and the crystal chandeliers were rising to the ceiling. There would be no more conversation until the first intermission. Tom was glad that there were two intermissions for this opera. When the act ended, neither of them stood up. They just picked up the conversation where they had left off. Fred told Tom where he lived.

"That's right off the highway I use to go home," Tom said. "I'd be delighted to drop you off. In fact, I could pick you up on the way into town for the next opera." Tom could not believe all the things he was saying. This guy could be an ax murderer for all he knew.

"That would be fantastic. Thanks.

"What do you do Tom?" Fred asked.

"I have a marketing business. We do marketing for new products; gizmos, food, whatever" Tom answered. "What's your line?"

"I'm a CPA and like I said I just got transferred to our New York office."

Tom decided to probe. "I got transferred from Buffalo to New York years ago, but I requested the transfer so it was not traumatic for me." Even though he was alone at the opera, it was possible that Fred's wife didn't care to go with him so Tom asked, "Was it hard for your wife and family to make the move?"

"No wife, no family," Fred said. "I'm a bachelor right now."

"Right now?" Tom noted. "Were you ever married?"

"Not exactly married, but I was in a relationship for about six years. I never could figure out why, but it all unraveled and fell apart."

"I'm sorry," Tom commented.

"No need to be sorry. These things are always for the best. How about you? Do you have a family?" Fred was the curious one now.

"Like you, I was in a fantastic relationship for nearly twenty years, but cancer ended it."

"Sorry."

"Thanks," Tom answered.

"So we are both bachelors," Fred observed, and he left it at that. They continued chatting until the intermission ended. When the second intermission began Fred asked Tom where the nearest men's room was.

"I'll show you," Tom said and they both stood up. There was a line at the bathroom and there were only three urinals and two commodes, so they did not end up side by side. Tom was done first and he waited outside the men's room for Fred to exit.

"Can I buy you a drink?" Tom asked, "Since I'm the designated driver."

"No thanks, I hardly ever drink anything stronger than a coke." They returned to their seats.

When the lights began to dim, Fred leaned over and whispered in Tom's ear, "I'm gay. You are too, aren't you?" Tom nodded and smiled at Fred.

And that's how it all began. When they reached Fred's apartment, Fred invited Tom up for coffee. "I really should get on home," Tom said, "but I need to exchange addresses and phone numbers with you so I can keep in touch until the next opera."

When they were inside Fred's apartment, Fred said, "I was really hoping that we could see each other before that. Would you have dinner with me tomorrow evening? I don't know anyone here yet and like they say, Saturday is the loneliest night of the week."

"Listen Fred," Tom said. "I have the greatest bunch of friends in the world. They have done their best to keep me from being lonely since Dominick died. I've put on a good act, and they think that they have been successful. I even have sex with some of them, but they have no clue how lonely I have been. Every Saturday evening we have dinner at a club in The Village and then we see the drag show. Do you think that you would like to join me, join us? I've been the odd man for a while now."

As he said that, Tom could see a tear forming in Fred's eyes. The two lonely men fell into each other's arms. Their lips met and their kisses became passionate.

"I haven't had sex in months," Fred informed Tom. "Do you think...."

Tom interrupted Fred. "Where's the bedroom?" he asked.

The two men stood naked facing each other before they got into bed. "You're beautiful," Tom said.

"So are you."

Tom instinctively knew that Fred needed this more than he did so he decided to take the lead. He applied Mac's definitive trip around the world until Fred had to beg him for relief. Fred spurted so much cum that as expert as he was, Tom lost most of it as it dribbled out of his mouth. When Tom came up for air, Fred hungrily devoured the drippings.

"That was fantastic," Fred said. "You are really great. Now it's my turn."

"Your turn is my pleasure," Tom lay on his back in anticipation.

And so Tom's life was renewed. Fred accompanied him to The Village the next evening and the guys really liked him. Fred and Tom knew that they were meant for each other the moment they met. That night the family's table was graced by two heavenly lights. After that evening in The Village, Fred accompanied the friends wherever they went, even to church. When Fred's lease was up, he moved into Tom's apartment. The family was now complete again.

As for me, I no longer believe in impossibilities. Everything is possible. Just keep on believing that you deserve the best that life has to offer, and it will surely come to you.

About the Author

Hank Brooks was born in Brooklyn, NY and lived most of his adult life in and around the New York City area.

He is very active in SAGE, a senior advocacy group for gay men and women.

He has three children and five grandsons. He is a retired CPA, and now lives with his partner, Leo, in Coconut Creek, Florida.

Hank Brooks is also the author of ***An Anthology of Erotica - Gay Love Stories*** and ***Fathers and Sons.*** Available at Amazon.com, TheNazcaPlainsCorp.com or your local bookstore.

AN ANTHOLOGY OF EROTICA
Gay Love Stories

by HANK BROOKS

BROOKS

AN ANTHOLOGY OF EROTICA: GAY LOVE STORIES

FATHERS
and SONS

a novel by HANK BROOKS

BROOKS

FATHERS AND SONS

A
BONER
BOOK

www.ingramcontent.com/pod-product-compliance
Lightning Source LLC
Chambersburg PA
CBHW051126260626
47170CB00005B/1689